My Lame Life:
Queen of the Misfits

Jen Mann

Throat Punch Media, LLC

Copyright 2017 by Throat Punch Media, LLC

All rights reserved.

This book is dedicated to Gomer and Adolpha.
You asked me to write a book you can read. Here you go!
Thanks for letting me embarrass you and I'm sorry your life is so lame.

Tuesday
July 5

So, it was Taco Tuesday and there I was, sitting with my family at a table for four at Dos Hombres and shoving tacos (with a side of chips and guac) in my piehole like it was my freaking job when my dad ruined my life.

Well actually, I didn't exactly hear him ruin my life at first. I think it was all the crunchy goodness drowning him out or the fact that since the age of twelve I've simply lost interest in most everything my parents say to me—seriously, I haven't heard a full sentence out of either of them for two years now. All I know is all of a sudden I felt the eyes of my entire family on me and my mom said, "Well, goodness, Plum, you sure are taking the news so much better than I thought you would."

And I was all, *The news? What news was I taking so much better than she thought I would?* I figured it was probably some new feminist cause she was railing about. We don't have much in common, but Mom can always count on me to yell, "Women belong in the house … and the Senate!" any time she brings up the wage gap or banning public breastfeeding or whatever new atrocity she's yelling about. My mouth was too full to yell, "Down with the patriarchy!" so I said, "Huh?" and I sort of spit chewed up chips across the table.

"Oh man! Plum, you are so gross!" yelled my brother Pax.

Pax and I are twins, but you'd never know it to look at us. I'm shorter and squatier and bustier than most girls our age. Mom says I got the "Parrish chest." Neither my grandmother nor my aunt have normal-looking figures. They've got shelves where everyone else has boobs. They could hold a cup of tea on there—and a book. I haven't tried holding tea on my shelf yet. I just try to keep it all under wraps as much as possible. Sports bras really keep that situation under control, but Mom says they give me uniboob. She's desperate to take me bra shopping and get a real fitting, but I refuse. It's not natural to let a stranger into a dressing room with you when you're topless. I don't want some old woman who smells like talcum powder fondling my funbags. And besides, no amount of lifting and separating will help me. I've seen Grandma Parrish naked. I was five at the time, but the image is still burned into my brain and it will probably stay there until I die. Boobs to her knees. Her knees, I tell ya!! She could throw them over her shoulders if she wanted to. She straps herself into a contraption that looks half straightjacket/half parachute and it doesn't help one bit. I'm going my own route on this one. I'm convinced if I wear *two* sports bras it will keep my shelf from growing. So far it hasn't worked, but I'm not giving up yet.

I've got frizzy, curlyish, brown hair that can only be described as "mousy." It hangs in my face most of the time. Mostly because I don't know what to do with it. I have a blow-dryer, but drying my hair takes forever. Who has time for that nonsense? I much prefer to spend those twenty minutes sleeping in rather than fighting with my hair, especially when I know it's going to be a losing battle. I can blow-dry it and within half an hour it's frizzy again. It's a hopeless cause. I'm ghostly pale—seriously, like NO tan lines anywhere, it's actually kind of weird, because I go outside … sometimes … so you'd think I'd have a tan line here or there, but nope. I think it's because Mom is obsessed with SPF and I believe a hat covers a host of hair problems, so I'm rarely without sunblock or a hat. No amount of SPF keeps me from freckling though. My only source of color comes from my full-body blanket of freckles. And without my glasses, I'm squinty.

Pax is tall and his physique can only be described as "strapping." He has shoulders that look like they belong to a man rather than a fourteen-year-old boy. His blond hair is perfect. He comes out of the shower and towels off his hair, shakes his head twice, squirts what I can only assume is some kind of miracle gel in his hair, and his waves simply fall perfectly and naturally into just the right spots. (I tried that once and my cowlicks ended up looking like two furry mice fighting to the death on the top of my head.) He has a year-round tan that makes his blond hair and blue (20/20, of course) eyes stand out even more.

I'm sullen and easily agitated, whereas Pax is cheerful and easygoing. Mom says I'm a cat and Pax is a dog. Whatever. If you ask me, dogs are dumb. They eat their own poop, for goodness' sake.

I've repeatedly asked for DNA testing to be done, because I'm pretty sure there was a mixup at the hospital. Since I have the Parrish chest I know I'm legit, it's Pax who doesn't fit with *me*. I'm convinced my real twin is being raised by a family of Norwegian supermodels next to a fjord somewhere.

"Stop it, Pax," Mom said. "Leave your sister alone."

"Yeah, leave me alone," I sneered, grabbing another chip.

"Plum," Dad said. "You haven't said anything. So, you're cool with all of this?"

All of this? What the blazes was he talking about? Obviously this wasn't about gender equality. "What are we talking about?" I asked, shoving the chip in my mouth.

Dad sighed heavily and shook his head. "I knew you weren't listening to me."

"You never pay attention, Plum," Mom said.

"We're moving, Plum!" Pax said, throwing a chip at me.

Wait.

What?

Come again? Whadidyasay?

We're moving? Like, away from here?

SHUT THE FRONT DOOR! How on God's green earth did I miss that memo?

"We're moving?" I sputtered. "To where?"

And then all of a sudden everyone in my family was talking at once. Something about how I never pay attention and I never take out my earbuds and I don't listen carefully or whatever. (Honestly, I'm not sure about the specifics because I wasn't listening that closely to them yell at me.) But in my defense, it was *TACO NIGHT*. I was a little preoccupied with my meal. And Dad drones on. All. The. Time. Of course I tuned him out. Ninety-nine percent of what he says has no bearing on my life. It's always stuff about working up to my potential and cleaning up after myself. How was I supposed to know he was telling me something vitally important? *LIKE, WE'RE MOVING!* He should have snapped his fingers or clapped his hands for attention so I would have known I needed to take out my buds and tear myself away from my delicious Tower of Tacos and listen to him. Sheesh!! Everyone was acting like somehow this was MY fault or something.

"Well, I thought you took the news awfully well, Plum," Pax said. "Makes perfect sense now."

Of course I took the news well. Mostly because I didn't hear the news! What a crappy way to tell your kid you're basically ending her life. And what a *sneaky* way to tell us. You know the parental unit had probably known for days but they waited until Taco Tuesday to tell me and Pax just so they could sneak the news in under our radar. They wanted to soften the blow and have us distracted by spicy, cheesy, crunchy goodness. The peasants are always happier when they're fat and happy. If they'd told us on Meatloaf Monday, you know there would have been a full-on revolt.

At that point there were a lot of tears and crying. (It was all me doing that, BTW. Apparently my whole family—Pax included—is excited for a "new adventure!" Ugh, yeah, how exactly am I related to these people?) I don't remember a lot of what was said, but basically, my dad's been working his tail off and he snagged a promotion with his company and the way they're rewarding him is to move him to KANSAS.

Kansas? Really? That's a place where people actually live?

WAAAAHHHH! News flash, Dad, no one thinks Kansas is an upgrade from New Jersey. Your boss obviously hates you.

After I calmed down (and comforted myself with more chips and guac), Mom gave a speech about looking on the bright side of life or whatever. I swear, that woman thinks we live in a Broadway musical or something.

So, this is happening. In one month I will be a resident of Kansas. What's in Kansas, anyway? I'm thinking farms, cows, and twisters. Maybe a few brainless scarecrows and wicked witches.

This is sooooo unfair. I'm starting ninth grade in the fall. Freshman in high school. My BFF Kennedy and I have already picked lockers right next to each other. We also bought matching tops for the first day of school. They're black—our signature color. We were going to be co-leaders of the French Club and plan the French Club trip to Montreal in the spring. I don't even know if Kansas has high schools. Maybe they're one-room schoolhouses like Laura Ingalls Wilder went to? Oh my God! Maybe I will have to be homeschooled! I can't even imagine Mom trying to teach me and Pax math. That woman can't do math unless she's trying to figure out 60 percent off a pair of stretchy pants at Marshalls.

Everyone sat there grinning at me and I wanted to yell, "Is this real life? Someone wake me up, because I think I'm having a fever dream!"

So. There it is. Life. Officially. Over. And now Taco Tuesdays are ruined for me. Screw you, Taco Tuesday! You're dead to me now.

Oh, who am I kidding? Nothing could ever ruin Taco Tuesdays. I can't quit guac. But I'm pissed Mom and Dad at least tarnished Taco Tuesdays for me, for at least a month or so.

When we got home from Dos Hombres, Mom inexplicably handed me a gift. On the outside I tried to be all, "A gift isn't going to fix anything. I'm still at mad at you," but c'mon. It was a present. So on the inside I was all, *Whaaaaaat? A present? For me? Whoohoo! I love presents. Thank you, Mommy!*

I mean, who doesn't like presents, right? Actually, my dad doesn't really like presents. He feels like whatever he needs he'll just buy and if he doesn't own it already, then he obviously doesn't need it. I know, I know. It's like the dumbest logic ever, right? One time Mom and I went Christmas shopping for him and we bought him this coat Mom showed him the week before. She thought he needed a new coat since he's worn the same one for twenty years. I'm not even joking. Twenty years. It was super ratty. The right sleeve was coming detached from the rest of the coat and the lining was ripped in the back and hung down and flapped like a stringy flag in the wind. Dude needed a new coat, but he refused.

"I love this coat," he told Mom, petting his raggedy-ass coat. "It's finally worn in and comfortable now."

Mom wasn't having it, so she bought the new one. We were leaving the store and he called her on her cell phone before we'd even reached the car. "I see a credit card purchase at Macy's," Dad said. "Take the coat back. I told you last week I don't need a new coat."

Mom stood there for a good five minutes trying to decide what to do. She was furious and she was ranting so loudly people were staring at us. An old lady asked me if I needed help or something. "Do you know this woman, honey?" the old lady asked me. "Are you safe?"

I nodded my head. "Yeah, we go together," I assured the helpful old lady. "She's just having a moment."

Finally, Mom took the coat home, wrapped it, and put it under the Christmas tree with the receipt stapled to the tag. "It's the thought that counts," she said all snippy-snappy when he opened it. "If you hate it so much, then *you* return it."

That coat is hanging in the front hall closet with the tags and receipt still attached. Dad refuses to wear the coat because he doesn't "need" it, but he's also too lazy to drive to the mall and return it.

I'm nothing like Dad (well, except maybe for the lazy part). I love presents, so I was excited when Mom said she had a present for me. I was really hoping Mom had bought me a new pair of Chuck Taylors. I've been dropping hints for weeks and I was thinking maybe I'd finally gotten through her thick skull. I closed my eyes and held out my hands, hoping she'd picked a cool color; otherwise it was going to be soooo awkward when I asked her to return them. *Meh. It'll be fine,* I thought. *I'll tell her they're the wrong size or something and spare her feelings.*

Anyhoo, instead of dropping a shoebox in my hands, I got a book.
Huh????

It was like a for-real paper book. Don't get me wrong, I like to read, but when your parents have rocked your world and they're trying to make up with you by giving you a present and so you're really hoping for new kicks and you get a book instead, it's a fairly big letdown. Like super-sad-trombones sad. *Wah-wah.*

Mom could see I was disappointed, so she tried to do that whole phony excited thing moms do. "Ooooooh, loooook," she exclaimed, stretching out every word and opening her eyes really wide. She turned the book this way and that like it was some kind of jeweled treasure that would catch the light.

It didn't.

Besides, that kind of crap only works with toddlers and really old people like my grandma.

But I'm not a monster, so I humored her and took a closer look. The book she was displaying wasn't really a book. It was a blank book. *What a useless thing,* I thought. *What good is a book you can't even read?* It had a purple leather cover embossed in silver with the words: DON'T FORGET TO BE AWESOME TODAY!

"Yeah," I said. "It's a blank book."

"No," Mom said, flipping the pages dramatically. "It's a *journal.* A plum-colored journal for my Plum." (PS—My mom has this *thing* about buying me purple things: hairbrushes, phone cases, stuffed animals, stationery. I get it. My name is Plum; plums are purple, but *stahp* already. It was kind of adorable when I was five, but now it's starting to get weird. Also, I hate the color purple. A lot.)

I was all, "A what?"

And then she told me this long-drawn-out story about how when she was my age she used to keep a notebook where she wrote down all her hopes and dreams and fears and poetry (that I assume was terrible), and blah, blah, blah. Honestly, I lost track of what she was saying about halfway through her speech. I was thinking about how I needed to text Kennedy and tell her how lame my mom was for buying me a blank book instead of Chucks. I don't even know what Mom was thinking. What possessed her to buy such a relic? When was the last time she saw me write anything on paper? Maybe when I was eight I wrote my spelling words down or something. I can't even remember the last time I wrote on paper—that's how long it had been. It was as if she didn't even know me. In my mind I was picking out just the right puking emoji to send Kennedy when I heard Mom sigh heavily and say grumpily, "I don't know, Plum. I just thought it would be fun for you to keep track of what you're feeling with the move and everything." She pouted.

"What I'm feeling?" I said. "Oh, that's easy. I feel like killing myself."

"Don't be so dramatic, Plum," Mom said. "We don't joke about suicide in this house."

I groaned. "Okay, I feel like breaking something. I feel like kicking a wall or throwing a vase. I feel like screaming. I feel like you and Dad must hate me."

Mom's eyes welled with tears and she walked away before I could see her cry.

Great. Suddenly I was the jerk. What was I supposed to do with that book? Write down my deepest darkest thoughts and my most intimate feelings or something? Ugh. Hard pass. That sounded like torture.

Why would I do that? *Who* would ever read it?

My class buried a time capsule last year. It's supposed to be dug up in thirty years—or maybe it's fifty?—either way we're going to be super old when they dig it up. There are letters in there from everyone and copies of newspapers and magazines so the people of the future can see what the past was like.

I figured maybe I should treat Mom's journal like a time capsule. So here I am writing in it, assuming whoever reads it (besides my snoopy mom, of course) will know nothing about me. Maybe by then I'll be living in France with my ridiculously handsome and smart French husband and a couple of precocious *bébés*. Or maybe I'll be scaling Mt. Everest. Or maybe I'll be working on the cure for cancer. Oh, who am I fooling? I won't be doing any of these things. I will most likely be a cat lady or a lunch lady.

Oh balls!

What if I'm a lunch lady *with* a lot of cats!?

Jesus. I can't think about that or else I'll get so depressed I won't want to leave my room. Nope. I'll go ahead and say when someone finds this journal and reads it, I'll be famous. I'm not certain what I'll be famous *for* exactly, but something amazeballs, that's for sure. And I can guarantee I *won't* be famous for owning a bunch of cats.

It might have taken my parents two times to tell me we're moving, but the message got through. Loud and clear. So, thanks a lot for the journal, Mom. I'm so glad I have a place to document the END OF THE WORLD. Especially since I have no hopes and dreams anymore, because you and Dad *SHATTERED* them.

It's obvious my parents hate me. They didn't even talk to me and Pax first. They just made the decision and *then* told us. We've always had a democracy in our house. Every Friday night we eat dinner out and we vote on restaurants, majority rules. We can't even order an appetizer unless everyone is in agreement, but they can move us cross-country without so much as a consultation?

So, let me get this straight, we can't order mozzarella sticks unless I pay Pax two bucks to say yes. (He always wants potato skins. Barf. Everyone knows cheese tastes better deep fried and smothered in red sauce rather than swimming in a boat made from the dusty skin of a potato.) But my parents can sell my house, pack up everything I own, and move me across the country without even so much as a warning, let alone a vote?! Yeah, that seems fair.

I was so upset about the whole thing I actually started writing in this dumb blank book. I can't say I feel better, but I definitely don't feel worse, so I guess that's something, right?

Mom says I can write all my feelings and whatnot, but I can't swear in this journal, which is stupid, because she and Dad could get awards for their swearing. No joke. They don't do it much in front of me and Pax unless they're really mad, but when they think we can't hear? Whoa! They could make sailors and truckers blush. Mom always says I need to broaden my vocabulary first and *then* I can swear. *Le sigh.* She also told me I can't have any expectations of privacy. This book is mine, but she can read it any time she wants. She said it was for my own safety—yada yada. She said if she catches me being "inappropriate" in my journal (or on my cell phone, or on my computer, or whatever), I'll lose my privileges. Sometimes being a teenager really sucks. On one hand Mom and Dad are like, "You're old enough to know better, Plum," but then on the other hand they're like, "You're too young to do that, Plum." I just can't win.

And was her threat supposed to scare me? Screw that. I don't care anymore. Mom and Dad have lost their power over me. What would they really do if I dropped an F-bomb in my journal? Ground me? From what? Kansas? Okay! Please *fucking* do!

Mom wants me to use this space to write down my feelings. Well, my feelings aren't all sunshine and puppy dogs. I'm pissed off. But I've always been pissed off. This is really not a new emotion for me. I think I was born pissed off. Sure, I'm mad about moving to Kansas, but everything irritates me. I get mad at people who post pictures of their post-workout selfies on Instagram—we get it, you worked out before I even dragged my lazy ass out of bed, you (very fit) twit! I get mad at guys who say "dude" too much—I can feel my brain cells literally die when I'm around those dudes. I get mad at the people who get mad when they aren't wished the holiday of their choice in December. Someone said "happy holidays" to you—don't be a dick, how hard is it to just say, "You too"?

What I'm trying to say here is I'm an angry, ranty girl and my feelings are going to be harsh! Mom says writing stuff down always makes her feel better, though. She's angry and ranty, too, but she says she has to control it in public or else she'll get arrested. "I write so that I don't hurt anyone—accidentally, of course," she says. She might be on to something with this book. Maybe this blank book thing is the best thing for me. Normally I find myself blurting out completely inappropriate things and getting myself into trouble. Writing this stuff down might be good for me. It will be like therapy, but cheaper and I won't have to put on real pants (Mom says as she much as she'd love it, pajama pants don't count as real pants, which I disagree with completely, but I digress) and leave my house to talk to someone—because I hate talking to people more than looking at post-workout selfies.

I think my journal needs a name, but what should I name it? Plum's Diary sounds so boring. Hmm … Picking Plum's Brain? *Blech*. Pondering Plum? *Snooze*. Plum's Perspicacity? *Possibly*.

I know! I've got it.

My Lame Life by Plum Parrish. This book is going to need some punch lists, too. Don't worry, I'm not really violent. I talk tough, but I've never actually punched anyone in my life, not even Pax. I just like the idea of making a hit list. It makes me feel better.

So, going forward this journal will document my whole miserable existence.

PS—I sure hope my mom is snooping right now, because then she'd know what I think of her and Dad. Hi, Mom! Don't be mad about the F-bomb—at least I'm writing in this dang thing!

Plum's Punch List:

1. Dad
2. Mom
3. Dad's stupid company
4. Kansas

Wednesday
July 6

I woke up hoping last night's dinner at Dos Hombres had been a bad dream. I mean, not the Tower of Tacos, just the part where they told me I was moving to Kansas.

It wasn't a bad dream. The move to Kansas is still on the calendar Mom has hanging on the fridge. Circled in red. Glaring at me. Taunting me.

When I went down for breakfast I could see Mom has already started packing. She says Pax and I have to help today, but I have plans to hang out with Kennedy. Mom says I should invite Kennedy over to help me. Oh yeah, that will go over well. I can only imagine: "Hey, Kennedy. What are you doing today? Pool day? That sounds awful. Why are you doing that? My mom says skin cancer is a killer. You don't want to die, do you? Hey, I know! I have a much better idea! Wouldn't you rather come over and help me box up my sweaters? It's almost like I'm saving your life or something. I'm that kind of a friend, Kennedy. You're totally welcome."

Ugh. Riiiiight.

I went to check on Pax and he already had close to half his closet boxed up. He is such an overachiever. "What is wrong with you?" I demanded.

"What do you mean?" Pax asked. "I'm packing."

"But *whyyyyy?*" I whined.

"I'm meeting the guys at the movies, so I got up early to get my work done," Pax said, stacking shirts neatly in the box at his feet.

"We need to stop this. You and I," I said.

Pax frowned. "Stop what?"

"The move. Kansas. All of it."

Pax shrugged. "It's a done deal, Plum." He stopped working and looked at me. "I would think you'd be happy."

I was shocked. "Why would I be happy?" I screeched.

Pax shrugged. "I dunno. I wonder why you think it's so great here. You don't really…y'know…fit in at school."

"What are you talking about?"

"I mean you really only hang around Kennedy and Madame O'Malley, your French teacher. I just thought maybe you'd like a change of scenery. You could maybe reinvent yourself. Be someone new." He did a halfhearted jazz hands thing. BTW, my family loves jazz hands. I have no idea why. So flipping weird.

"Reinvent myself?" I was so confused. What the heck was he talking about? Why would he say that to me? Is there something wrong with me?

Pax sighed heavily. "Look, Plum, I love you. Mom and Dad love you. But you do know you're a … difficult girl, right? You're a handful." My jaw dropped, practically to the floor, but Pax either ignored me or didn't see, because he kept going. "You're loud. You say whatever is on your mind. And you're a little weird too. You always have been. People don't know what to think of you most of the time. Everyone here has known you since preschool and they all know your…quirks…and they don't easily forget. You've either offended everyone or they think you're crazy. Kansas might be a nice change for you. You can start a new school and be anyone you want. Y'know…quirk-free or whatever."

I was absolutely stunned. I tried to take it all in. What did he call me? *Difficult? A handful? Loud? Weird?* Oh, and lucky me, now I've been given a second chance and I can finally be quirk-free? Is that what he is saying? I could feel tears pricking my eyeballs, threatening to spill over my lashes. I always cry when I'm mad. It's a terrible reaction, which just makes me madder and the tears come faster. I fought back the tears and tried to keep my voice calm when I said, "I am not a difficult girl, Pax, or loud. I'm just not like you and your friends: sheeple! Like today. What movie are you seeing with *your boys?*" Pax shrugged, completely indifferent. "Exactly. You have no idea. Because you don't care. You're slow-witted. You just go with the flow. You have no strong opinions about anything! You'd see a chick flick if Big Bro in Charge said so. You've got your nose so far up Big Bro's butt that you don't even know who you are. You guys stalk the school halls in packs because you're afraid to be alone. You can't handle the silence of your own thoughts in your head. You dress like the mannequins at the Nike store, because there's not one original thinker in the bunch. I don't need to move away and reinvent myself, Pax. But maybe *you* do!" I tried so hard to keep my voice calm, but I was screeching by the end of my speech.

"Wow. See? No filter, Plum," Pax said, shaking his head.

"Leave me alone!" I kicked over his box of shirts and ran away before he could see I was crying.

Be anyone I want? Can you believe he said that to me? I want to be ME! Right?! Don't I? I mean, I think I do. I'm not perfect, but I'm not horrible either…I think? Jeez, Pax made it sound like maybe I should be embarrassed of who I am. I've never even thought about being embarrassed of myself. It's never occurred to me—until now. Shit. Who knew Pax felt that way about me? My own brother. My own twin! Thanks a lot, Pax.

He thinks I should want to change, huh? Into what? Someone more like him? No, thank you! I don't want to be like Pax. I don't want to roam everywhere with my lookalike posse clearing a path for my procession. I don't want to talk about the latest vapid celebrity naked selfie or the coolest footwear offering from some idiot sports star or yuk it up with the lugs he calls friends. I don't need a bazillion people to hang around me to make me feel like I'm someone special.

But…I had no idea the kids at school thought I was difficult or weird. I mean, I'm not stupid. I know Pax has more friends than me, but I'm not sure when that happened exactly. Don't get me wrong, I love hanging out with Kennedy, and Madame O'Malley is *incroyable*—both as a French teacher and a mentor—but I thought keeping my circle small was my own choice. I really imagined *I* was the one turning down invitations to go to parties or the movies or dances. I can see that those kinds of invitations stopped a long time ago.

I guess they stopped because I'm difficult.

And loud.

And weird.

And a handful.

When we were really little, Pax and I would both get invited to our classmates' birthday parties, but then in second grade, I stopped getting invitations. Only Pax got them. Second grade must have been the cutoff when the moms decided their kids didn't need to invite everyone in the class. I always told Mom and Dad it didn't bother me when Pax had a birthday party to attend almost every weekend and I didn't, but if I'm being honest, it *did* bother me. It hurt my feelings a lot, but I'd shove those feelings down. I refused to think about the fun my brother and my classmates were having without me. I told myself birthday parties were dumb and a waste of time. Mom tried to do something special with me while Pax was gone, but getting mani-pedis with your mom isn't near as much fun as spending two hours roller-skating and eating cake and ice cream.

Wow. So, I'm difficult … and loud … and weird … and a handful. Good to know.

Plum's Punch List:

1. Perfect Pax
2. Birthday parties
3. Mani-pedis

Thursday

July 7

I pitched a fit tonight. It wasn't pretty, but in the end I think it was worth it.

I thought a lot about what Pax said to me and I decided maybe I could make some small tweaks. So, I told Mom I wanted to reinvent myself when we moved to Kansas. I told her I wanted to go to the mall and buy whatever was on the mannequin at the trendiest store there. I told her I wanted to quit French Club and join the cheerleading squad. I really should have said soccer team or something, because I'm probably the only fourteen-year-old who still can't do a roundoff, but I blurted it out before I could really think it through. Meh. I can be the base of the pyramid or whatever. They're always looking for stocky girls to anchor their pyramids or hold them up and stuff and Dad likes to say I'm "strong like bull," so I can totally handle that.

I thought Mom'd be happy. I thought she'd be excited to finally have two normal kids. Instead, she freaked the freak out. Like, BIG TIME.

"Why do you want to change?" she wailed. "You do you, Plum!"

Mom is really into self-empowerment. Especially for me. She thinks girls have a harder time with self-esteem than boys. I once overheard her tell Dad that Pax was so confident he was a borderline narcissist and she was working on some insults she could throw his way to knock him down a peg or two. Dad said if she was belittling their kids, add me to the list because I was bossy.

16

Mom said I wasn't bossy, I had leadership skills that just needed to be honed. Dad sighed heavily at that one.

"I thought you'd be happy!" I said. "I want to be a Stepford child."

Dad snickered. "It's Stepford *wife*."

"Whatever. Anyway, Pax said—" That's as far as I got before Dad yelled for Pax.

"We don't talk about members of our family without them here to defend themselves," Mom said while we waited. I rolled my eyes, because this is what I live with. I'm all for justice and equality and all that jazz, but sometimes I just want to talk shit about someone behind their back, y'know?

Pax came into the living room dribbling a soccer ball. "S'up?" he asked, never taking his eyes off his ball.

"All right, Plum, *now* tell us what Pax said," Mom said.

"Pax said I'm difficult and a handful and weird and loud and I need to reinvent myself in Kansas. Basically, I need to be more like him."

Pax stopped dribbling. "I never said you need to be more like me," Pax said.

"Well, that's what you meant!"

"No, it's not! What I meant was you just need to tone it down, Plum. You're so freaking intense. Everything is drama, drama, drama with you. Look at this. Right now. We're having this huge discussion because I was trying to help you see that you're A LOT to handle and then you missed the point entirely and ratcheted up your histrionics. You can't take any sort of criticism or feedback. Everything is a line in the sand with you. Either we're with you or we're against you. THIS is why no one likes you!" He blew one perfect curl off his forehead in exasperation.

I wanted to snatch that perfect curl out by its roots. "No one likes me?" I whispered.

"No one except Kennedy, but she's just as crazy as you are."

"That's enough, Pax," Dad said quietly. "You may go to your room and think about what you just said to your sister."

Pax huffed off. I could tell Pax wasn't going to think about anything except which YouTube video he should watch next.

"Plum," Mom said, patting the couch beside her. "Sometimes your brother doesn't think before he speaks."

"Yes, he does," I said, sitting down heavily.

"Pax is an idiot," Dad scoffed.

"Pax is a straight-A student, Dad. If anyone is the idiot, it's me. I'm the C student."

Mom stroked my hair. "That's just because they don't give out grades for being awesome."

That was when I started crying and I couldn't stop. I don't even know why I was crying. I think it was partly because what Pax said hurt me. He's the only person whose opinion I actually care about. Pax has never been mean to me on purpose, but lately he hasn't been nice to me. He didn't even try to sugarcoat what he said. I think I was also crying because I knew Mom and Dad love me a lot, but sometimes that just isn't enough. When your brother has told you twice in two days everyone at your school thinks you're weird, the love of your parents isn't really going to keep you going. You know? And knowing everyone thinks I'm A LOT to handle or whatever made me appreciate Kennedy so much more, but in less than a month I'll have to leave her and hope I can find a new Kennedy. So I was bawling about that too. And I was also crying because I was thinking about my goldfish, Mr. Bubbles. I got him for Christmas when I was five and by New Year's Eve he was gone. I got up in the middle of the night to go to the bathroom (too many sparkling grape juice toasts at midnight) and I stepped on something slimy and squishy. I screamed like a goat and flipped on the light. There was Mr. Bubbles laying lifeless on my carpet. He'd committed suicide by jumping out of his bowl. He hadn't been with us for long, but I was attached to that blasted fish and sometimes when I'm sad about other things, I think of Mr. Bubbles and I get even sadder. It's stupid, I know, but that's how I'm wired. Shut up.

Mom and Dad talked me down and assured me they would do whatever they had to do to help me have an easy transition to Kansas.

"What can we do?" Dad asked.

"Simple," I replied, wiping away the tears. "Don't take the job."

Mom and Dad exchanged a tired look and Dad said, "I can't do that,

Plum. Someday when you're older and you have a family to take care of you'll see that there are hard choices you have to make. This is one of those choices."

"I know! We could go tomorrow and get mani-pedis!" Mom suggested.

Oh my God! Why does Mom think mani-pedis will solve all the world's problems? I bet she thinks peace in the Middle East could be brokered over mani-pedis. "I'm good on mani-pedis," I said wearily.

"Look, Plum, if you want to reinvent yourself or whatever, we can help you," Dad said. "What do you think you need?"

I considered his question. What would make a difference? A more outgoing personality? A filter? A friendlier demeanor? A less shelflike chest? None of those things seemed achievable. If I was going to reinvent myself I needed to be a better version of me. What does Mom always say? *You do you, Plum.* She wants me to be myself and not conform to anyone else's ideal. Maybe I need to embrace my A LOT-ness and just really go for it. I need to make a statement and let the world know I'm not messing around. I could be the cool eclectic girl who doesn't give a fuck what anyone thinks. The kids at my new school would be drawn to me because I would be mysterious and confident—a girl comfortable in her own strange skin.

The only problem is I'm not comfortable in my skin. I'm going to have to work on that.

I ran a hand through my hair. *My hair*, I thought. I've always hated my hair. I could start there. That would be an easy enough fix and it could be the jumping-off point for my whole new sassy, confident look. So I said, "A haircut. My hair sucks."

Mom pet my head. "Your hair is beau—"

Dad cut Mom off with a sharp look. "Find a picture on the Internet and your mother will take you," he said.

"And I want to dye it pink."

When I said that Mom's eyes popped out of her head like a cartoon character. Just like those ones that say, *"Awoooooga! Awoooooga!"* It was kind of like that, except silent, of course, and her eyes stayed in her head, but you get my drift.

Dad kept it cooler. "Pink?" he asked, all casual.

"Yeah."

"Sweetie, I thought you were trying to blend in with the other kids?" Mom squeaked.

"Yeah, I don't think I'm going to do that. You're the one who tells me to be me. I'm not like anyone else, Mom. And I don't want to be. I may not like myself a whole lot, but I'd definitely hate myself if I changed to be like the other girls in my school. Pax is right. I can use this move as an opportunity to change. Only, I'm not changing how I think or act. I'm going to change how I accept myself. I'm going to embrace who I am. I'm going to own my 'a lot-ness' and change into the real me. The real Plum Parrish. The real Plum is a girl with pink—not purple, Mom—but pink hair."

Mom got tears in her eyes. "You do you, Plum," she said, pulling me close.

And now as I sit here writing this, all I can think is: holy crap, what if Mom's stylist effs up my hair and turns it orange or something? I'll literally die. Confident, cool Plum has pink hair, not orange. Deep breaths, Plum. You'll get through it.

Plum's Punch List:

1. Mousy hair
2. Mani-pedis (enough already, Mom)

Saturday

July 9

My hair is pink!!!!!!!!!!!!!!!!!!!!! It is a glorious shade of bubblegum with cotton candy highlights and just a hint of strawberry.

I also got a supercool haircut. All shaggy and flippy and messy. *BUT ON PURPOSE.*

My stylist called it "piece-y" and said I needed a flat iron, so Mom bought me one. It cost as much as three mani-pedis. I wasn't sure she was going to do it at first, but after she saw what magical things it could do, she said she'd buy it if I'd share it with her.

OHHHH. EMMMMM. GEEEEEE. Why did it take me so long to get a flat iron? Actually, I know what took me so long. Frankly, I was terrified. See, I watched a YouTube video of this girl who was showing you how to do *ah-may-zing* hairstyles with her flat iron. She had music on and she was rocking out while she was wrapping her hair around the iron. Then she pulled the flat iron out of her hair, and all of a sudden, a *smoking* chunk of her hair fell on the table in front of her. It was practically on fire. She had literally burned off her bangs. Like to the nub. Her roots were smoldering and she was screaming and then the video just ended. I have no idea what happened after. How do you fix burnt bangs? How do you come back from millions of people laughing at your dumb ass? I was like, HELLLLLL NO will I ever use a flat iron! Because I say things like, "My hair couldn't look any worse than it already does," but I'm lying when I say that. Smoldering tufts of hair will always look worse than two furry mice fighting on the top of my head. A hat can't hide that mess.

Anyhoo, I'm not worried this will happen to me because the stylist taught me how to use my flat iron properly. What heat setting to use and how long to leave it on my hair, that sort of thing. I only wish I'd had the guts to ask for instructions years ago, because this hot little number has changed my life. I can beat my cowlicks into submission with that thing. And since Mom's hair looked a thousand times better too when she tried it, she went and bought her own because she didn't want to share. #winningsohard

Even Pax had to admit I looked cool like this. Well, he didn't actually admit it. He just shook his head and said, "Pink? *That's* toning it down?" But he didn't say it looked bad, so I think he liked it. He's just jealous he doesn't have the confidence for pink hair. Poor guy.

To show my gratitude to Mom, I vowed to pack ten boxes today. Kennedy said she'd come and help. Apparently she LOVES packing. Who knew????

Plum's Punch List:

1. Nice try, Universe, but today was a great day

Monday

July 11

Kennedy totally lied about loving to pack. She doesn't love to pack. She loves to dig through your stuff and get easily distracted by every shiny object she comes across.

All day long all I heard was:

"Ooooh! Remember when we went to the Ren Fest and got ribbon wands! I loved these. Let me show you my moves, Plum."

"OMG! You saved this huge stack of *Seventeen* magazines all this time!? Check it out: 'What is He Really Thinking When He Doesn't Text You Back Right Away?' and 'Take the Test: Are You Date-Worthy?' Come on, Plum. Let's take the test!"

"Legos! There's a whole bin of Legos under the bed, Plum. Let's build something, pleeeeeeeeease. I haven't played with Legos in, like, forever."

Kennedy was worthless in the packing department, but she did remind me of how much fun we've had together over the years. She has been my only friend since kindergarten. How was I going to find another Kennedy in Kansas? I don't have to try with Kennedy, she just understands me. I can't even think about finding new friends. The thought literally sends me into a panic. We don't have enough paper bags for me to breathe into.

So, today I tried to pack twenty boxes. Mom says I don't even have twenty boxes of stuff.

I might if I take my ribbon wands and Legos and all the other toys in the back of my closet.

Mom wants to have a garage sale and get rid of a lot of our stuff. She says it's expensive to move it and we don't need it anymore.

Pax has a whole bunch of things he wants to sell: Halloween costumes, stuffed animals, sports equipment he's either outgrown or abandoned (like his week-long obsessions with badminton and bowling), baseball cards, and books (he might be a smart kid, but Pax throws out books every chance he gets—he's positively beastly).

I had sorted my things into "Pack," "Donate," "Sell," and "Trash" piles when Mom came to check on me.

She took one look at my enormous "Pack" pile and asked, "How's it going, Plum? Do you need some help in here?"

I shook my glorious pink tresses and said, "Nope."

"I don't see much to sell, donate, or trash," Mom said, poking through my collection of Garbage Pail Kid cards.

I snatched the cards away. "That's because I'm keeping a lot of my *possessions*," I said. "I want to continue to *possess* these things."

Mom pursed her lips and tipped her head at me. "I get it, Plum. It's hard to part with some of this stuff. You're stuck in two worlds. You're at an in-between point right now. You're part little girl and part big girl."

My mouth dropped open. How. Dare. She. *Little girl?* Did she really say that out loud to me? I have pink hair. I dare her to name one little girl with pink hair (who isn't a cartoon character)! I am not a little girl.

Besides, I wasn't saving what she perceived to be nothing but clutter because I'm a child. Those Garbage Pail Kid cards are retro treasures! I saw a whole documentary about a guy who makes his living selling old toys online. He pokes around rummage sales and finds hidden valuable "junk" he then sells for serious bank. My room is full of the same paraphernalia he was selling. I could totally be worth a lot of money someday. I wasn't positive, but I was guessing those Garbage Pail Kids were collector's items. And wouldn't Mom be glad I saved them when they ended up paying for my college tuition!?

Sure, I hadn't played with Legos since…well, since Kennedy was over a few days ago…and before that it had been a few years, but Legos are timeless. *Adults* play with Legos. My stuffed animals hadn't been cuddled in years, but they each have a story. I remember when I got each one of them: Ella the Elephant was from the Bronx Zoo; Louie the Lobster was from our road trip to Maine; and Dad brought home Simon the Snail from the Atlanta airport. Those were my childhood memories Mom was asking me to discard!

I decided to deflect her attention from me. "Pax is getting rid of Blankie," I said.

Mom looked so sad I actually regretted my words—but just a little bit. "I know," she said.

When we were born, Pax and I came early and we had to stay in the special nursery in the hospital for a few weeks. Mom never left us. She moved into a broom closet or something. Seriously. She said the hospital didn't have any available rooms. They wanted her to go home, but she refused, so they put a cot in a broom closet for her. There were brooms and mops and a big sink and a little bed for her to sleep on. She'd come and visit us in the nursery when she could, but there were a lot of times when we couldn't be disturbed. So while we rested, Mom sat in her broom closet and knitted blankets for us. When we finally came home, Mom wrapped us up in our blankets. There are pictures of us in our car seats bundled under the blankets Mom made. After that Pax and I took our blankets everywhere. We even named them. Pax named his Blankie and mine is Humina. I don't know why I named it that. I was like two or something and not very bright, obviously. I've slept with Humina every night since I was born. If I go to sleep over at Kennedy's house, I stick Humina in my pillowcase so I can still secretly stroke her soft nubbiness before I fall asleep. I just assumed Pax did the same thing, so I was shocked to see Blankie in his "Sell" pile.

Mom can have my ribbon wands, but she will have to pry Humina from my cold, dead hands. Humina will be with me on my wedding night— guaranteed. Unless that's weird. Is that weird? That's kind of weird, right? Hmm. We'll cross that bridge when we get to it, how's that?

"Are you going to sell Blankie?" I asked.

"No," Mom said, shaking her head. "I'm keeping Blankie if Pax doesn't want him."

"I'm keeping Humina," I said softly.

She reached out for me. "You keep whatever you need to keep, Plum. We'll move it all if we have to."

"Dad won't like that. He says we're paying the movers by the pound."

"I love your dad, Plum, but he is one cheap guy—and he's moving us to Kansas. Ignore him. Pack whatever you want."

After she left, I decided I didn't need the stack of *Seventeen* magazines. I looked up Garbage Pail Kids on eBay and found out they're worthless. I added those to the "Trash" pile with the magazines. The Legos are selling like hotcakes, though, so I went ahead and listed a few sets. Might not pay for college, but I could definitely earn enough to buy a new phone or something. Plus, the more I throw out or sell, the less I have to pack. That sounds great to me, since I ran out of steam after five boxes. I took a quiz instead. Turns out I'm not date-worthy. Is anyone surprised?

Plum's Punch List:

1. Packing
2. Packing
3. Packing
4. *Seventeen* quizzes

Thursday
July 14

OMG, we have so much stuff to get rid of!! The trash man is going to hate us. We've piled so much stuff on the curb it's embarrassing. But just when I thought *I* was embarrassed, I saw Mr. Jenkins from across the street digging through our trash. Yeah, he was poking through our castoffs. I watched him through my bedroom window. I saw him take my desk chair with the broken wheel and Pax's bookshelf that no longer has any shelves because when he got his black belt in taekwondo he used the shelves to show off his board-breaking skills to his friends. He is absolutely clay-brained sometimes. I'm not a black belt, but those crappy shelves were pressed wood; even *I* could have broken them. Mr. Jenkins also took a moldy plastic shower curtain from the trash pile. I wanted to open the window and yell, "That's our trash, Mr. Jenkins! What are you doing?" but I didn't because he's kind of terrifying.

He's so freaking weird and scary. I'm always checking those online neighborhood watch sites where child molesters have to register and stuff. I'm positive Mr. Jenkins is going to show up on there one day. He's probably already on the list but he's living across the street under an assumed name so we won't know. Oh my God. What if that's actually true? What if he is doing that? It's probably good we're moving away.

Pax says Mr. Jenkins is not a child molester. He thinks he's one of those quiet homicidal maniacs who buries bodies in his basement. Pax says we'll end up on the five o'clock news saying something like, "Mr. Jenkins? A murderer? Wow. I would not have guessed. He was always so quiet and kept to himself—except when he was digging through our trash, that is."

Pax is probably right. One time we were behind Mr. Jenkins in line at Walmart and he was totally buying serial killer materials. He had a long piece of rope, zip ties, tall rubber boots, a full-on plastic hazmat-looking suit, tarps, a chainsaw, and a shovel. The checkout girl asked him what he was working on and he said he was planting a garden. Ha! A garden! As if anyone was going to believe that one! I've never seen him plant anything in his yard. I must have scoffed a little too loudly, because he turned around and made eye contact with me. "Well, hello there, neighbors," he said, pretending to be friendly. Meanwhile, he has barely spoken to me in all the years we've lived across the street. A few times when he saw me at the mailbox he reprimanded me for letting my dog poop in his yard. I was like, "What are you even talking about, Mr. Jenkins? We don't own a dog, you nut bar!" The nut-bar part was in my head, but the rest was out loud.

Mom's always nice to Mr. Jenkins. She says he doesn't give her a creepy vibe at all, so she answered him. "Hi there, Mr. Jenkins," she said. "How are you?"

"Oh, I'm well, thanks. Just getting some things together for…uh…my garden. Yeah, I'm starting a garden. Maybe I'll surprise you with some tomatoes one of these days!" He smiled, but his eyes didn't smile, y'know what I mean? They just kept watching me, daring me to argue with him or something. He was right about one thing: tomatoes would be the most surprising things I'd find in his yard. And a human skull would be the least surprising.

He's a total serial killer. I shudder to think what he's going to do with my chair and shower curtain.

One good thing about moving away is I no longer have to worry Mr. Jenkins will someday bury me in his backyard.

Plum's Punch List:

1. Mr. Jenkins

Saturday
July 16

Today was our garage sale. I had to work it with Dad. He said we would run the sale if Pax and Mom continued packing. Mom seemed to think that was a good deal, so of course I felt like I got screwed. It was hot in the garage and I would be forced to deal with a bunch of cheapskate strangers while Pax worked in the air-conditioned house and probably took about a hundred breaks for cold sodas and snacks. I didn't have any choice, though. It had been decided. Once again, another decision I was not privy to. This is getting old!

Dad was all gung ho when I joined him out in the garage. "This is going to be fun, Plum!" he said. "Let's face it, we're the salesmen of the family. We have a knack for this kind of stuff. We're going to make so much money. Mom and Pax will be shocked."

I was skeptical, because everything we were selling could be classified only as junk and nothing was worth more than about two or three dollars. How in the world did he think we would make a fortune? Did he have a stockpile of gold somewhere he hadn't told me about, because Mom's used flip-flops weren't going to bring in loads of cash.

"Can't we just set fire to this crap and buy a new one of everything when we get to Kansas?" I whined.

"Now, now, Plum," Dad chided. "Where's your can-do spirit?"

"It's too early in the morning for can-do," I argued. Did you know garage sales start at eight in the morning? People were waiting outside the garage door when we opened it. Who does that? Do they not have a life or something?

The early risers were milling about and poking through our stuff when Dad pulled out a Sharpie and started changing the prices on things.

"Wait. What are you doing?" I asked him as he marked a pair of rollerblades up from two dollars to ten.

"I'm going to teach you about supply and demand," Dad said, scratching out the price on a skateboard.

"Umm, this is a garage sale, not the mall, Dad. I don't think supply and demand applies here."

"Oh, you'd be surprised, Plum. Check it out." Dad nodded at an older couple coming up the sidewalk toward our driveway. "Watch and learn."

"Hello," the man called from the end of the driveway. "Do you have any crockery?"

Huh?? Crockery? What the hell is crockery, right? I didn't know and neither did Dad. He looked at me just as confused. I shrugged.

"No," Dad called back. "I don't believe we do. But we have some wonderful wares. You should check us out! Come on in and take a look!"

"No, thanks," the woman yelled. "We're only buying crockery."

"Hang on!" Dad looked at the bowling ball in his hands. "Do you bowl much? This one's a beaut!" Yeah, he said "beaut," as in short for beautiful. Dad is the cheesiest salesman ever. I knew right then and there it would be the longest day of my life and no matter how much money we made it wouldn't be enough to make up for the lost time. Those were hours of my life I'll never get back.

The couple grumbled at one another and walked back to their car.

"They didn't even give us a chance," Dad complained, placing the *beaut* bowling ball on the floor. "And we have so many good things. How rude!"

I was trying to listen, but I was kind of hyperventilating because Brandon Phillips had just stepped into my garage. "Oh my," I said, like an old Southern woman with the vapors. Brandon Phillips is probably the most popular boy at my school. He's been the most popular boy since kindergarten. I don't know how that happens. It's like everyone looks at one kid and says, "You are the chosen one. You shall be popular until the end of time." I don't even get it. I mean, he's cute or whatever, but there are tons of cute boys at my school. He's not very smart and he tries to be funny, but his jokes are lame as shit. But still, he's *Brandon Phillips*. You have to swoon when he enters your airspace, it's like the law or something. I don't know. I don't make the laws, I just follow them.

"Hey, Plum," Brandon said.

"Heh," I grunted. It was all I could get out. I did not think Brandon knew my name.

"Hello, young man," Dad said. "I'm Plum's father."

I tried to communicate silently with Dad, *OHMYGODSHADDUP!!*

"Hey," Brandon mumbled, completely uninterested, of course.

I finally found my voice. "My hair is pink!" I announced.

Brandon looked at me. "Oh yeah, it sure is. Is that, like, on purpose, or...?"

"Of course it's on purpose. M-my-my mom paid a lot for it," I stuttered.

"Okay, cool. It's really...um...bright." Brandon nodded. "Is that a thing now? To have pink hair?"

"Yeah, it's a thing. For sure, it's a thing," I said, and then I made this weird *smack* noise with my lips, like a pop. *What the hell, Plum?!* I was failing miserably. Why do I talk out loud? I mean, honestly, I sound idiotic every single time I open my mouth. I looked to Dad, hoping he'd rescue me. But he just stood there, staring at me. If Mom had been there she'd know what to say. She would have complimented me on my hair or said she saw one of the Kardashians wants to go pink, too, or something. Anything! She would not have it go down like that.

Say something, I begged Dad silently.

He got the message.

Sort of.

"Looking for anything in particular?" Dad asked. "I've got a bowling ball here. It's a—"

I tried to use my telepathic skills once again, *Don't say beaut, don't say beaut, don't say beaut.*

"Pax said he's got his rollerblades for sale," Brandon interrupted.

"Yeah, they're right here." I held up the rollerblades.

Brandon took them from me. Our fingertips grazed and I almost giggled. *Keep it together, jingle brains!* I screamed in my head.

"How much?"

"Twelve dollars," Dad said.

Brandon was confused. "The sticker says two and ten?"

"Yeah," Dad said. "It's two plus ten. They're twelve. It's math, kid. It's not that hard. Do you want them or not? We've got other customers."

I looked around our empty garage. "Well, I'm pretty sure they're on their way," I whispered.

Brandon frowned. "I only have ten. Will you do ten, Plum? For me?" He dazzled me with his smile. Honestly, I would have done free at that point, but then he winked. Winked! Winking is a big deal, right? People don't just go around winking at random people. You only wink at the ones you care about … the ones you … LOVE! This is the point where I went off the deep end. I was positive Brandon Phillips was in love with me and I went on a tangent! I was like, it all makes perfect sense. He's probably been keeping his love a secret all this time hoping I'd make the first move, but when I didn't and he heard I was moving to Kansas, he knew he had to do something drastic. So he came over to my garage sale under the guise of wanting Pax's old rollerblades, but when he saw Dad was here guarding me, he needed to send a message. That's what the wink was! The wink was him saying, "I love you, Plum. Don't leave me." Look, I'm not proud of this ridiculous train of thought; it made complete sense at the time. I blame the heat and the fact I didn't eat breakfast. I was woozy and obviously hallucinating.

Once I was done fantasizing about my elaborate wedding to Brandon Phillips, I stammered, "Yeah, sure, of course. Yeah. Totally ten."

Brandon grinned. "Totally ten it is, then." And then he broke the spell. He did the grossest thing I think I've ever seen. He pulled off one tennis shoe and reached down into his sock and dug out a damp, sweaty, crumpled-up ten-dollar bill. "Here you go."

EWWWWWWWWWWWWWWWWWWWWWWWWW!!!!

I wanted to yell, "Are you kidding me right now? What kind of bumpkin carries money in his stinky sock?" I couldn't even keep my face neutral. It's a good thing I hadn't had breakfast that morning, because I would have puked it right up on that moist ten.

I looked completely disgusted when I said, "Just drop it on the table. I'll get it later."

Brandon shrugged. "All right. See you around, Plum," he said.

"Yeah, bye," I replied, still reeling from the stench of his feet. He threw another wink over his shoulder as he sauntered out the door. My stomach turned. Poor Brandon Phillips. He'll just have to pine for me, because that steamy ten-dollar bill was an absolute deal-breaker. There is no redeeming himself in my eyes after that transaction. Blech.

"That kid is disgusting," Dad said a little too loudly. "You should have held out for the twelve bucks and that would have never happened."

Dad and I spent the rest of the day wheeling and dealing. We sold dishes, curtains, rugs, and a ton of books. He even sold his golf clubs. They weren't even for sale, but a lady offered him fifty bucks and Dad couldn't resist making a sale. A lamp got broken when a woman with a giant purse knocked it over. Looking back now, I think that was a diversion to keep us occupied while she robbed us. We were busy cleaning up the broken lamp while she shoved costume jewelry in that giant purse of hers. I can't be certain it was her, but before the lamp broke the box of jewelry was there and after the lamp mess was cleaned up, the lady was gone and the box was empty.

"You gotta be smart, Plum," Dad lectured me. "We just lost eight bucks, because people suck and we're easily distracted."

"Shhh," I scolded him. A woman and her toddler were coming our way. I didn't want her to think all we did was complain about our customers. I decided to take the lead on this one. "Hello! Welcome!"

Dad wouldn't be outdone. "Hi there!" he said. "Looking for anything in particular?"

The woman looked perturbed that both Dad and I had spoken to her. I could tell she was feeling hassled. We were like those women in the lingerie department who hound me to let them measure me for a bra. "No, we're just browsing if that's okay," she said.

"That's fine," I said. "Take your time and let us know if we can help." I dragged Dad to the card table and chairs set up at the back of the garage. "Let the woman browse," I hissed. "You want something to drink?"

Dad sulked in his chair. "Yes, please."

I went in the house to get us drinks and when I got back Dad told me he needed to go in and use the restroom. "Keep an eye on that one," he whispered loudly, jutting his chin at the toddler. "We've got another thief."

"Dad!"

The woman spun around. "Excuse me?" she demanded. "What did you say about my daughter?"

"She's a little thief. Check her pockets, they're lined with Legos," Dad said.

"My child is not a thief," the woman said. "She's three!"

"Well, your three-year-old has sticky fingers," Dad said.

"This is unbelievable!" the woman cried. "Come on, Darby. Let's leave this mean man's house."

"Turn her upside down and shake her before she goes," Dad said to me as he headed into the house.

The woman dug in her child's pants and found several Legos stuffed in the pockets. "Mine!" Darby screamed. "Mine!"

"No, Darby, they're not yours," the woman said, dumping the pilfered Legos on the floor.

"Well, they could be," I said weakly. "For three dollars."

"I don't want to buy any more toys," the woman said.

I didn't know what to say. *Okay, so don't buy the toys, but don't take them either?*

"I don't see what the big deal is," she said. "It's just a couple of Legos."

"Yeah, and they're only three dollars," I said. "That's actually a really good deal on Legos. They're usually a lot more expensive than that."

"MIIIIINE!" Darby screeched.

That kid had absolutely no volume control. It was maddening. Why do people have kids? They're so annoying.

"I know, baby," the woman cooed at her brat. "You love those Legos, don't you?" The woman glared at me.

34

Like I was denying her kid or something! Seriously? What was I supposed to do? I was beginning to feel like a total jerk demanding money from a baby, but come on, it was THREE DOLLARS! Those Legos were worth a ton more than that. I glanced back at the door, hoping Dad would come out and rescue me. I needed his help. I couldn't fight with an adult. That would be disrespectful. But on the other hand, this woman wouldn't let it go.

Just then Madame O'Malley glided into the garage. (I say "glided" because that's really how she moves. She's so graceful it's like she floats everywhere she goes. It's ridiculous.) "*Bonjour!*" she said, gliding over to me so she could kiss both my cheeks—French greeting style.

"*Bonjour*, Madame," I said.

Darby's mother interrupted us. "Fine. I guess we'll take the Legos," she said. "Do you have change for a hundred?"

I looked at the shoebox serving as our cash register. It was full of crumpled one-dollar bills and a few random quarters. I was not prepared to break a hundred. "Umm …" I said, poking in the box, hoping there was a twenty hiding in there somewhere. All I could see was Brandon's limp ten, and I was never going to touch that thing again.

Madame O'Malley could see I was floundering. "How much are the Legos?" she asked.

"Three dollars," I said.

"Here you go." She handed me three crisp one-dollar bills.

"Oh, uh …"

Darby's mother grabbed her kid and the Legos and bolted out of the garage. "Thanks, lady!" she yelled.

"You didn't need to do that," I told Madame O'Malley.

She waved away my protests. "It's fine. I don't mind. I didn't want you to lose the sale."

I love Madame O'Malley. She's easily the kindest person I know. "Thank you," I said.

"*De rien,*" she said.

"I wish you hadn't, though. That woman was a nightmare," I grumbled.

"Now, Plum, that attitude isn't going to help you make friends in your new school. What do I keep telling you? You've got to find the positive in people."

I sighed. "Yeah, I know. Mom says that too. But it's sooo hard. I really don't like people. Especially people like her and her tiny monster, *Darby*."

Madame O'Malley got all serious and took hold of my shoulders so I could face her fully. "Plum, you are a special girl who feels everything so strongly. I would never want you to change, but I do want you to at least be aware of it. You are—"

I cut her off. "A lot to handle. I know."

Madame O'Malley smiled. "Yes, you are a lot to handle, but there is also a lot of you to love. You are fierce in your convictions and loyal to your friends. You are confident in your opinion and you are unafraid to share it. That might intimidate some people, and so you need to be aware of that. That's all I'm saying. If you want friends—and I think you do—then you need to be more aware of the vibe you're giving off. People are attracted to what you offer them. If you're offering sullen and morose, then that's what you'll attract."

I shrugged, because honestly, I'd rather be surrounded by a bunch of sullen and morose people than a bunch of shiny, happy people. I love Madame O'Malley, but she just doesn't get it sometimes. Sullen and morose people actually *feel* things. We don't pretend like everything is hunky dory when it's not. We don't put on fronts and happy faces while deep down inside we're screaming in agony. At least with me, people know what they're going to get. It was too hard to explain to Madame O'Malley, so I just said, "*Merci, Madame.*" Because that was really all she wanted to hear.

Dad came out of the house. "Did you get your Legos back, Plum?" he asked, not even noticing Madame O'Malley.

"No. I sold them."

Dad looked impressed. "Well done."

"Meh, Madame O'Malley bought them for that snotty kid." Madame O'Malley squeezed my arm gently and I fixed my tone. "I mean, Madame O'Malley bought them for that *spirited* little girl."

"Oh yeah? Well, thanks for that," Dad said, nodding at Madame O'Malley.

"I should be going," she said. "Good luck, Plum. Please keep in touch and let me know how you're enjoying Kansas. *Au revoir*."

"*Au revoir*, Madame," I said and kissed both of her cheeks. "Thank you for …" I hesitated, because what could I say? Thank you for being my friend, trying to help me fit in, teaching me a new culture, *getting me*? There was so much to thank her for, but I simply said, "…everything."

For a second we both just stood there and I could feel tears starting to prick my eyes and I was trying so hard not to cry. How stupid would that look? Crying over a teacher? Ugh. *Comment horrible!* Not to worry, though, Dad hates awkward silences and displays of emotion, so he did one of his usual bizarro silence-fillers. "Did you need any bras, Madame O'Malley?" he asked. "My wife has a bunch I'm supposed to take to a women's shelter later today, but if you could use them, I'm happy to give them to you. You look about her size."

Why do we let him speak to people?

Madame O'Malley graciously declined (BECAUSE, OF COURSE SHE DID) and quickly left.

"She sure was in a hurry to get out of here," Dad said.

"Yeah, because you offered her Mom's busted bras!"

"I didn't try to sell them to her. I was offering them for free!" Dad argued.

Plum's Punch List:

1. Sweaty money
2. ~~Bratty~~ Spirited kids
3. Saying goodbye to Madame O'Malley
4. Dad

Wednesday

July 20

Mom and Dad are in Kansas for a house-hunting trip. They called today to tell us they made an offer on a house. Mom was super excited because she's positive they found the perfect house for us. It's a quick commute to work for Dad and a great school for me and Pax.

It looks like this is really happening. I realize we've packed, sold, donated, or thrown out almost everything we own, but I was still hoping maybe Mom and Dad would be like, "Surprise! We were just kidding! We wanted you to clean out your closet for real this time and we thought this was the only way to get you to do the job."

Unfortunately that was not the case. They said they made an offer on a four-bedroom, three-and-a-half-bath home on a cul-de-sac.

"What's a cul-de-sac?" I asked.

"It's fancy for 'dead-end street,'" Dad said.

"I think it's French," Mom said. "Cool dee sack. You should ask Madame O'Malley."

"I doubt it," I replied. "What color is it?"

"What? The cul-de-sac?" Dad asked. "It's the same color as the roads in New Jersey. Kind of gray."

"Oh my God, Dad! No! The house." I mean, of course the streets are the same color. Duh! Did he think I was some kind of moron who didn't know what color streets are?

38

"Sorry," Dad said, all miffed. "I would call it beige."

"No," Mom argued. "I think she called the color Sand. Or maybe it was Buff."

"Isn't that what I said?" Dad said. "It's beige."

"The Realtor called it Camel," Mom said.

"Beige?" I asked. Our house in Jersey is blue with a yellow door. "Not blue?"

"We didn't see one blue house here, Plum," Mom said.

"Yeah, it's like there's a law against color or something," Dad said. "Every house is a different shade of beige."

"We saw one that was greige," Mom said.

I ask you, what the hell color is greige?

"The kitchen was terrible in that one."

"Yes, it was," Mom agreed.

"Okay, no one cares. Stop talking about greige houses you didn't buy," I said.

"Is there a yard?" Pax asked.

"Yes, of course," Mom said. "There's even a basketball goal that stays with the house. So you can shoot hoops or whatever."

"That's cool," said Pax. "All right, see you later." He got up to leave.

"Wait," I said. "That's it? That's all you care about? We're uprooting our entire lives and you want to know if there's grass?"

"You asked what color the house is. Who cares what color it is, Plum? Like your questions are more important than mine," Pax argued.

I didn't respond, because he kind of had me there. My question was as dumb as his. Sometimes he's the worst.

"You're both going to love it here," Mom said.

"Oh yeah?" I said, wondering what she could possibly say that would make me love Kansas.

"Yeah!" Mom exclaimed. "Because you know what I saw today, Plum?"

"What?"

"There's a place really close to the new house where we can go for mani-pedis."

"I gotta go," I sighed.

Sometimes I wish I was an orphan.

Plum's Punch List:

1. Greige
2. Fricking mani-pedis!!!!!!

Friday

July 29

It has been a flurry of activity since Mom and Dad got back from Kansas. We've been showing our house, trying to get it sold while trying to pack. Yeah, spoiler alert, I'm still not done packing. I might have a hoarding problem.

I haven't been able to see much of Kennedy, so I invited her over last night for one very last sleepover before I move away. I want to say it was *ah-may-zing*. That we had so much fun and stayed up late into the night promising to be best friends forever no matter what, blah, blah, blah. But it didn't go that way. Not at all.

Kennedy seemed off all night long. She was distracted and even a bit irritable with me. She argued with everything I said and made a point to tell me several times just how immature and babyish I am. I heard a lot of: "We're going to be in high school, Plum, stop acting like a middle schooler!" and "Why are you always so embarrassing?" and "How do you even function in real society, Plum?" It was pretty rough. I pretended to fall asleep at nine because I couldn't take the jabs anymore.

I wasn't sure what was going on with her. Looking back now, I realize she's changed a lot over the summer. In eighth grade, Kennedy was an outsider like me. She had a bowl cut and glasses and acne. She was so flat-chested boys would bump into walls and say, "Oh, excuse me, Kennedy."

41

High-larious. Over the last few months, Kennedy changed. Her hair is growing out, she got contacts, and the acne is almost completely gone. And the boobs. Oh my God. The boobs. Like, ridiculous boobs. Mom even noticed. "Wow. Kennedy is really budding this summer!" she said. Budding? More like blossoming right into a C-cup.

I don't think it's the budding that's causing Kennedy's mood swings. I wanted to chalk up her awful behavior to her realizing how much she was going to miss me—like she was lashing out because she was so torn up inside but didn't want me to know—however, I quickly realized that wasn't it at all. When she was in the shower this morning, her phone chirped and I could see a new text message had come through. It was from Melissa Hodges. I was sort of confused why Kennedy was getting text messages from Melissa, because we're not friends with Melissa. I mean, she's okay, I guess, if you like vapid, brain-dead, boy-crazy girls. It's a well-known fact Melissa stuffs her bra and she's one of those girls who plays dumb around boys. Girls like that make Gloria Steinem want to burn stuff down—I assume.

I hated to snoop, but I was worried maybe Melissa had been kidnapped and she was texting everyone on her contacts list for help. That was the only plausible reason I could come up with. I couldn't very well ignore a plea for help. I convinced myself I was doing good when I punched in the passcode and opened Kennedy's phone. We took an online safety class in sixth grade and we were told to use a passcode that was easy to remember but hard to crack. Kennedy used my birthdate and I used hers. We actually thought it was pretty genius of us. Thank goodness she hadn't changed it. I opened the text message. It wasn't the first one Melissa had sent. I could see that a conversation had started just after Kennedy arrived and had been taking place all night long.

MELISSA: WHERE RU? A IS HERE LOOKING FOR YOU!!

KENNEDY: HE IS? SRSLY?!

MELISSA: YES!

At that point, I had so many questions. Like, who is "A" and why is he looking for Kennedy? And why is Melissa the one to tell her? When did they get so close? *I* am Kennedy's BFF. Where did this interloper come from? I was trying to think of the last time I saw Melissa and Kennedy together. It was, like, third grade or something. I remember we had a spelling test and Kennedy asked Melissa if she could borrow a pencil and Melissa told Mrs. Batchelder that Kennedy was cheating and Kennedy got a zero and after that Melissa was dead to us both. When did things change? How did I miss the memo Melissa and Kennedy were hanging out together?

I had to keep reading. I needed more intel.

KENNEDY: TOLD YOU. I HAVE TO SLEEP OVER @ PLUM'S.

MELISSA: WHY??????

KENNEDY: SHE'S MOVING.

MELISSA: A WHOLE NIGHT WITH PLUM PARRISH? POOR YOU. I CAN'T EVEN.

KENNEDY: EH. IT'S OK.

Whoa, Melissa was a bit harsh. At least Kennedy stuck up for me, though. I mean, well, she kind of did. I was a little worried at first. I was afraid maybe she was going to throw me under the bus, but she sort of came through for me. I kept reading.

MELISSA: IF YOU SAY SO. PARTY IS RAGING. UR MISSING GOOD ONE.

KENNEDY: I FIGURED. SOOOOO BUMMED.

MELISSA: RU AT LEAST HAVING FUN WITH THE PURPLE PEOPLE EATER?

Purple People Eater? Are we six or something? That was Melissa's best insult? *Yawn.*

KENNEDY: LOL. WHAT DO YOU THINK?

Umm…ouch!?

MELISSA: FIGURED.

KENNEDY: ALSO, SHE'S A PINK PEOPLE EATER NOW.

MELISSA: ??

KENNEDY: SHE DYED HER HAIR PINK.

MELISSA: STFU. FOR REAL?

KENNEDY: SHE LOOKS LIKE PINKY PIE.

MELISSA: PICTURES OR I DON'T BELIEVE U.

KENNEDY: GTG. SHE WANTS TO BRAID MY HAIR OR SOMETHING.

MELISSA: OMG! SOOOOO WEIRD!!!!

KENNEDY: IKR?

Damn! Looked like Kennedy grew boobs *and* an attitude this summer! What was happening? Was I in *The Twilight Zone*? Where was Kennedy, my best friend? She said she liked my hair. She was even thinking of dyeing hers too, but her mom said no. I decided to give Kennedy a pass. It could have all been sarcasm. After all, sometimes it can be hard to infer tone in a text message. Maybe she really did think I was interested in braiding her hair. Obviously going forward I need to be more clear about what I have planned when I invite her to a sleepover. Also, Melissa is a total hag.

MELISSA: OMG!! A WANTS TO ASK YOU OUT. HE JUST TOLD ME.

KENNEDY: HE DOES?? OMG, THAT IS CRAZY!

MELISSA: YOU MUST GET HERE. TELL PLUM UR SICK OR SOMETHING.

KENNEDY: NAH. CAN'T DO IT TO PLUM. CALL ME TOMORROW AND GIVE ME THE DEETS.

See??? I was so relieved to see I was right. Kennedy would never diss me. She and Melissa might be newish friends, but we're BFFs. We have an unbreakable bond. No one can come between us.

MELISSA: BIG MISTAKE.

KENNEDY: PROBABLY.

Wow. Ouch. That stung.

I'd just finished reading the whole exchange when I heard the shower shut off. When Kennedy emerged from the bathroom, toweling off her dripping hair, her phone was exactly where I'd found it and I was casually flipping through a magazine.

Her phone chirped and she immediately checked it. She got a huge grin on her face, but then it disappeared when she saw me looking at her. "What's up?" I asked, trying to look interested in the magazine. I was sure it was Melissa updating her on the mysterious A situation.

She put down her phone and grabbed her comb. "It's my mom," Kennedy said. "She's so lame. She said I have to come home right away so I can babysit Lincoln." She rolled her eyes so convincingly I almost believed her.

"I could come too," I offered. "It's my last day. We could hang out and do something fun with Lincoln."

Kennedy looked aghast. She's always been a terrible liar. "Nah, it would be so lame for you. Like you said, it's your last day. You don't want to hang out with me and my little sister. You should go have fun!"

And within fifteen minutes Kennedy was gone. Poof!

Aren't BFFs supposed to exchange matching necklaces and cry or something? Needless to say, it wasn't at all what I expected.

I should have never snooped in Kennedy's phone. It was private and I had no right to peek. It totally hurt my feelings to know I've sort of been replaced. I don't know when Melissa entered the picture, and I was shocked to see what Kennedy was saying to her about me. It serves me right for being so nosy, but it was still super rude. And who is "A"? And why all the drama about this guy? What was he? Kennedy and I have never had crushes on boys. I mean, except for Brandon Phillips, but that's mostly because everyone else swoons over him and so we just swoon so that we're conforming. For the most part, boys are immature freak shows who say and do gross things and keep sweaty money in their socks. Since when did Kennedy put boys on her radar? I suddenly felt like an outsider in my own relationship with my best friend. Can that even happen?

Plum's Punch List:

1. Melissa Hodges
2. The mysterious Mr. "A"
3. Me, for being a snoop

Thursday

August 4

When the movers showed up today, the first thing Mom did was insult them. They were a husband-and-wife team, and they were both only an inch or two taller than me. Mom took one look at their diminutive frames standing on our front porch and announced, "Oh no. There must be some kind of mistake. We have heavy furniture. This isn't going to work."

The woman glared at Mom and pushed past her into the house. She walked over to a large wooden bookcase and gave it a nudge, rocking it a bit. She nodded, pulled out a long fabric strap, and slung it around the bookcase. She grabbed the ends of the straps, bent slightly at the knees, grunted softly, and pulled the bookcase over onto her back like a backpack.

"Let me help you!" Dad cried, rushing to her side.

"Back off!" the woman hissed in a heavy Eastern European accent. "I am professional." And then she sauntered out the door like she was carrying a sack of feathers instead of a 100-pound piece of furniture.

The woman, Olga—she told us her name at lunchtime when she took a break to eat the pizza Mom ordered as a peace offering—has been a professional mover for twenty years. Before that she was a dance instructor. She met her husband, Igor, when she needed a piano moved to a new studio she was going to open. She had no one to help her. She didn't have any friends or family nearby and she said her dancers were too weak to help. I don't know many dancers, but the few I do know are always hungry, so this didn't surprise me at all. Anyway, she needed some help, so she found an ad in the Yellow Pages (whatever those are) for a piano mover and when she called she got Igor. They immediately recognized one another's accents and discovered they were from the same Russian—or maybe it was Ukrainian?—city and even had some mutual friends. He agreed to come to her studio the next day. Around mouthfuls of pepperoni pizza, she said it was love at first sight. ("He has good butt!" Olga announced, giving Igor's rump a slap.) After he moved Olga's piano, Igor bought her dinner and told her it was his dream to have his own moving company someday, but he also wanted a wife. The only problem was he'd need to stay busy to be successful, so he'd be gone a lot. He needed a wife who could be his partner. She needed to be able to move pianos and such with him and travel the country. He said none of the women he'd met at that point wanted to travel so much. Yeah, I'm sure the traveling part was what women were opposed to, not the lugging sofas part. Olga sold her piano and her studio and she and Igor hit the road.

Olga was muscling a king-size headboard out the front door when I heard Dad whisper to Mom. "There is truly a lid for every pot, huh?"

Mom nodded and quickly scribbled something in the notebook she always carries. My guess is Mom's next novel will be some sweeping romance set on the open road about an immigrant couple who find love lugging strangers' refrigerators on their backs while helping one another study for the US citizenship test.

I was sitting on the porch watching Olga and Igor pack the moving truck like a giant game of Tetris when Kennedy showed up unexpectedly.

I hadn't seen her since the sleepover and I wasn't quite sure what to say, so I just said, "Hey."

I could see she was just as uncomfortable as I was. "Hey," she replied.

"What are you doing here?" I asked.

She shrugged. "You're leaving today, right?"

I nodded.

"I just thought I'd come by and see you before you go. Since…I don't know…I probably won't ever see you again," she said.

"Really? You don't think so?" I said. My chest constricted and my stomach turned. I hadn't really thought that through. I sort of assumed we'd visit one another over the summers and keep in touch until college where we'd be roommates and marry boy BFFs, buy homes next door to one another, and then name our first daughters after one another who would then grow up to repeat the BFF cycle and we'd share grandkids. Wasn't that what BFFs do? Even when they're long-distance BFFs?? And even when Melissa Hodges is vying to take my spot and there's something going down with the mysterious "A"?

"Well, yeah. I mean, I can't see me going to Kansas any time soon. Like, what's even there for me?"

I wanted to scream, "MEEEEEEEEEEEEEEEEEEEE!!!!! I'm there. Your BFF is there. You'd come to visit me!" but instead I shrugged and said, "Yeah, it's probably super lame."

"Super," Kennedy agreed.

"So…" I said. Seriously. It was so awkward.

Kennedy kept looking at her shoes and then finally she spoke. "Plum, you've been my best friend since…well, since as long as I can remember. You've always been there for me. I want you to know I might not have always shown it, but I appreciate you. You're what a friend should be like." And then she hugged me.

Wow. Finally, right?! Suddenly all the weirdness was gone between us. The text messages to Melissa and "A" didn't matter anymore. My BFF was back! THIS was how we were supposed to have said goodbye after the sleepover.

Sure, she might never come and visit me in Kansas or exchange matching necklaces with me, but we'd totally go to the same college and be roommates. It was a given now. Kennedy really is the lid to my pot. As soon as she left I was online picking out matching duvets for our college dorm room. I realize it's still a few years off, but I wanted to go ahead and start getting some ideas at least. I didn't want to leave something that important to the last minute, y'know?

Plum's Punch List:

1. Leaving my BFF

Sunday
August 7

Welp. I'm in Kansas. They really did it. It has been an insane few days. Let me catch you up.

Once the house was packed up, I went through my empty room one more time, trying to memorize the space so I'd never forget it. That room was the only room I've ever lived in. That's a big deal, people. I was kind of freaking out a little bit. Even Pax went outside and sat on our swing set one more time. That is not normal Pax behavior. The two of us were clearly distressed. But my parents tried to pretend like it wasn't traumatizing at all. Mom kept showing me pictures of the new house and blabbering nonstop about how much fun we were going to have (insert jazz hands here). I finally had to tell her to quiet down.

"If you use the world 'adventure' one more time, I swear to God, I'll run away," I said.

Mom tried to smush me in a hug. "I'd find you and bring you back," she said.

"Don't be such a grump," Dad said. "Embrace the chaos! Enjoy the ad—"

"That goes for you, too!" I said.

After that they left me alone. But are you really ever alone when your parents are in your airspace? Just the sound of Mom's breathing was enough to send me over the edge.

MY LAME LIFE: QUEEN OF THE MISFITS

We took an airplane to Kansas. I thought we would drive, but Dad said it was too far. Plus, we don't have a car anymore. Dad had to leave his company car in Jersey. They'll give him a new one in Kansas. Mom sold her Subaru. She said when she and Dad were house-hunting she noticed "everyone" drives either an SUV or a minivan. She said she wants to get a new car so she could "fit in."

Ha! Please let the record show I didn't believe her for a second. My mom doesn't give a lick about fitting in. She once wore a prairie skirt to a formal wedding. She proudly wears Crocs every day. She leaves rant-filled notes on the windshields of badly parked cars. She laughs louder than anyone I know, and she swears in church. Fitting in is not her thing. She just *wanted* a minivan. Always has. She's been begging Dad to buy one for years, but he's always resisted—he says they're lady mobiles. Like the Subaru was some kind of statement of masculinity or something.

Besides being an affront to his manhood, Dad also didn't want a minivan because they're gas-guzzlers. He despises anything wasteful. I knew Mom would win, though. She always does. After all, I saw her pack that winter coat with the tags still on it. He *will* wear it one of these days.

We approached the airport for landing and I craned my neck to see as much as I could. It was soooo flat. Like pancake flat. And desolate. I couldn't spot a building anywhere. Not even a house. Where does everyone live? Underground? I tried to remember if Mom and Dad said anything about our beige house being underground. I didn't specifically ask if it was above ground, I just assumed it was.

"Where are all the houses?" I asked as the plane touched down.

Mom shrugged. "There's so much land here that no one has to live near the airport. It's a bit of a drive to civilization, but so much better than living in a flight path, right?"

While I was waiting at the luggage carousel for our four identical black suitcases to drop down the slide, I eavesdropped on the conversations happening around me and tried to figure out what Kansans talk about. It really wasn't much different than what New Jerseyans talk about: gripes about sports, politicians, and their in-laws, just with a different accent. I saw a few

51

people sneak peeks at my hair and one woman snapped a picture with her phone. I was pretty sure she was going to show it to her stylist to copy.

I spotted an elderly woman standing next to me struggling with an enormous suitcase. I reached over and grabbed the handle. I channeled my inner-Olga, bent my knees, and hoisted the bag off the belt. "Here you go," I said.

"Thank you, dear," the woman said, patting my arm. "And I'm very sorry about your hair. I hope you can get that fixed."

Before I could say anything she was gone.

Pax snickered. "Come on, Strong Like Bull, let's get the rest of the bags and get out of here before someone starts a Go Fund Me for your hair."

Dad hailed a cab and our first stop was a car dealership where we bought…wait for it…a minivan.

Called it!

I must admit, once I hopped into our new suburban assault vehicle, I could see why Mom had been coveting a swagger wagon for so long. Pax and I each got our own row and I have at least five cupholders that belong solely to me. Plus, the slidey doors are the easiest ever. Why doesn't every car have push-button slidey doors? They're absolutely genius for lazy people like myself.

We had a few days to kill before Olga and Igor showed up, so Mom and Dad had a "surprise" planned.

Oh no.

Surprises are never good with those two. Something strange has happened over the last few years. It's like my parents have missed the memo that Pax and I are now teenagers. They think going out for a scoop of ice cream or hitting the newest animated movie with talking and singing animals is going to blow our minds. Last summer Dad took us to a model train show featuring Thomas the Tank Engine. Thank God there was no one there over the age of four or else I might have died from sheer embarrassment. I could only imagine what they had cooked up for us this time. I warned them that if the zoo was on their list of surprises, I would not be responsible for whatever I broke in my rage.

Silly me. The zoo would have been a lovely surprise compared to the actual surprise. We ended up at the one-and-a-half-star-rated Teepee Motor Lodge. It was as horrible as it sounds. Let me explain. It was a motel consisting of individual teepees clustered around a dusty courtyard with a pool in the middle. The main office was one giant teepee with a gravel road connecting it to ten smaller teepees where the guests stayed. Pax and I shared a teepee. Our round room had a tiny bathroom and a television that looked older than us. The focal points of the room were the two double beds that vibrated when you put quarters in a machine on the headboard. It took me about five minutes to realize the place didn't have Wi-Fi or cable television. Is that even legal? And, oh yeah, the "heated pool" the blinking sign out front boasted about was closed indefinitely for repairs.

Pax and I were considering running away and finding a new family when Dad knocked on our door. He came in all serious like and sat down on Pax's vibrating bed. (We'd plugged in about five bucks' worth of quarters before we realized neither of us really cared for the sensation.) Dad took off his glasses and rubbed his face. He looked beat.

"L-l-l-l-l-isten, ki-i-i-i-i-ids," he said. The bed shook violently. He groaned and moved over to my non-vibrating bed and tried again. "Listen, kids, I realize that this place isn't ideal. Your mom read about it in a magazine and thought it sounded like a hoot. Clearly, it's a tad outdated and a bit … kitschy."

"There's no Wi-Fi," I complained.

"The TV only has three channels," Pax whined. "And one of them is a 24-hour farm report."

Dad sighed heavily. "And the pool is out of commission. I know, I know. But here's the thing. Your mom was trying to do something nice for the two of you and if you ruin it for her, so help me…" he trailed off. I had no idea what that threat meant. Pax and I have never really been punished in our lives. And I'm the drama queen in the family. Ha. Dad could give me a run for my money. "I know you both think this move is hard on you, but it's also hard on your mother."

He could see I was skeptical. "You don't believe me? Where is she going to make friends, Plum? When you were babies, she joined support groups for new moms. Those are the kinds of places where your mom made her friends in New Jersey. You and Pax are too old for Mommy and Me music classes or the playground. There aren't too many mixers for moms of high schoolers. She can't let you know that she's worried or scared or upset, because she's being strong for the both of you."

Pax looked sheepish. I was still skeptical. My mom tells us on a daily basis how much she hates people. She thinks most of the people around us are ignoramuses who care more about what celebrities are wearing or who they're sleeping with than who our president is and what he's up to. Every time she sets foot outside of our house, she comes home railing against the stupidity of the sheeple she's encountered in the toothpaste aisle at Target. My mom doesn't need friends, because she doesn't want friends. If she wanted friends she wouldn't act like that, right?

I took a closer look at Dad and realized he looked spent. We were moving across the country for him, and it was putting a ton of pressure on him. He was feeling responsible for all our unhappiness. That wasn't fair to him. Maybe he wasn't exaggerating about Mom either. Maybe she was going to have just as tough a time adjusting as me and Pax.

"We'll *try* to be more pleasant," I promised Dad. "Right, Pax?" I nudged him.

He was already on his phone texting someone. "What?" he said, looking around, a little startled to see we were still in an enormous concrete teepee and still having a conversation he had no interest in participating in. "Oh, yeah, sure, Dad. Whatever you want."

Dad smiled. "Thanks, P-squared." He strangled us both in a giant bear hug. "Now, who wants to see a million sunflowers?"

I know what you're thinking right now: *Huh?*

Yup, THAT was the big surprise. *Surprise! We're going to look at a field of flowers!* (Jazz hands.)

I've really got to teach my parents what a surprise is. A surprise is getting me front-row seats to see Adele. A surprise is the hottest, newest phone with an unlimited data plan. A surprise is a shopping spree at the mall. A surprise

ISN'T a bloody blank book or a fifty-year-old (probably bedbug-infested) hotel room shaped like a stupid teepee or a field full of frigging allergens! My parents need to look up the word "surprise," because they clearly don't understand the meaning.

We drove out into the country—I mean, farther into the country than we already were—to this farm that has a million sunflowers. Dad wasn't exaggerating at all. Do you know what a million sunflowers look like? Sunflowers as far as you can see. They all stood in neat lines, swaying gently in the breeze under the bluest sky. I have to admit, it was a bit more spectacular than I'd imagined. A million sunflowers are kind of impressive, but there was no way I was going to let Mom know that.

I got my gaping under control while she ran around like fricking Pollyanna. It was like she'd never seen a field of a million sunflowers. Oh, wait…that's right, none of us had, but still. It was downright embarrassing to watch her. She wore this giant straw hat ("Because I'm so fair, Plum. I don't want to burn," she said, but really she's always looking for any excuse to wear that dumb hat in public) and carried a basket that she filled with flowers Dad cut for her. I'm not sure if she was acting out an actual scene from *Pollyanna*, but it sure felt like it. It could have been worse, I guess. There was another mom there who made her whole family dress alike and they had a professional photographer taking pictures of them posed in the flowers. They even had this old-fashioned sofa someone (The photographer? His overworked assistant?) had hauled into the field of sunflowers. At one point, I saw Mom notice them and I could see the wheels turning in her head.

"Don't get any ideas, woman," I whispered to her.

She smiled and threw an arm around me. "Oh, Plum, I always think it would be terrific to do something like that. Wouldn't we have some amazing photos if we did that? But then I think about doing that with *our* family. We don't even have matching clothes, so that would be our first hurdle. Dad would complain constantly about how much it was costing. Pax would only look up from his phone to whine about how hot he was and to demand, 'How much longer?'"

She was right. Completely. "What about me? How am I difficult?" I asked, nudging her.

Mom smiled. "You wouldn't actually complain out loud, because you're pretty good to humor me and my wild ideas. But I know you, and I'd be able to see how unhappy you were. You would be absolutely mortified to be dressed like the rest of us. And you would be humiliated to be on display like that. Look at us, we're gawking at that family and we're talking about them. You would *die* if people were watching you and talking about you."

I nodded. "And don't forget about my dead eyes," I reminded her.

She guffawed. "Yes, you and your dad's dead eyes would ruin my beautiful picture that I paid so much for."

I don't know what it is about me and Dad, but we cannot take a decent picture. We try. We really do. Mom yells, "Smile!" and then she and Pax break into the warmest and most natural smiles while Dad and I look like we're doing proof-of-life photos for kidnappers. Our bodies go absolutely rigid and we freeze in unnatural positions. Our eyes go wide and soulless and our smiles can only be described as grimaces. I haven't taken a good picture since I was four years old.

"Hey, Plum," Mom said.

I turned to look and she snapped a picture on her phone.

"Mom!" I grumbled.

"Look, Plummy, look how beautiful you are," Mom said, holding up the phone.

I looked. For a second I wasn't even sure it was me. The girl in the picture looked carefree and happy. Sunflowers framed her face, and sunlight glinted off her hair. She was smiling naturally and her eyes were bright and her cheeks were flushed.

I have to admit I looked halfway decent in that picture. I'm sure it was just a trick of the light. Or Mom has some new filter on her phone that makes everyone look a billion percent better than normal.

"Huh," I said.

"You look fabulous," she said.

"Psht," I said, pushing her phone away. "Anyone can look fabulous with a million sunflowers as a backdrop."

Plum's Punch List:

1. Sleeping in a concrete teepee
2. Vibrating beds
3. ~~1,000,000 sunflowers~~

Tuesday
August 9

I think it was around three o'clock in the morning when something hit me in the head. One minute I was sleeping soundly in my concrete teepee and the next minute I was half awake trying to understand what was happening. In my sleepy stupor, I thought Pax was throwing things at me. "Knock it off, Pax," I mumbled, swatting around my head.

"Whaaa?" Pax mumbled back.

I was drifting off when something hit my head again. Only it was harder this time. "Ow," I said. I rubbed my head. "What was that?" I honestly didn't know if I was more irritated I'd been woken up or that he was throwing stuff at me. I couldn't understand what was happening. My brain was still moving very slowly at that point. I didn't know what he'd thrown. It wasn't painful, it was just…odd. Sort of soft and hard all at the same time. Maybe a small pillow or something? I felt around blindly, but I couldn't feel anything on my covers. And then it happened again. The soft/hard thing hit me in the side of the head.

"Pax!"

"What?" Pax asked, flopping over, but still half asleep.

"Stop throwing things at my head!" I growled.

That's when I got hit again. This time it was in the chest. It bumped into my shelf and then I thought it fell on the floor.

"PAX! You jackhole! What the heck?" That one woke me. I was ready to get up and pummel him when I saw it coming this time. Only it wasn't a sock or a T-shirt or a pillow as I had originally thought. I strained my eyes in the dark trying to discern what I was seeing. There was something darker than the super dark room and it was floating near the ceiling. *Wait a minute,* I thought. *It's not floating; it looks more like it's gliding.* I fumbled around for my glasses so I could get a closer look. "What is that floating up there…?" I found my glasses and shoved them on my face, bringing into focus two beady eyes glinting in the moonlight. But they weren't floating or gliding. They were flying! And not just flying, more like dive-bombing. I still couldn't figure out what it was, but whatever it was, it was coming in hot and aimed right at my face! At the last second I realized the beady eyes belonged to a bat. A bat that was going to blitz my head like a kamikaze any second. "Oh my God!" I screamed, throwing the covers over my head just before the bat slammed into my face. It skimmed the sheet and I could feel its tiny feet tangle momentarily in the curly mess of hair that was sticking out of the blankets. Luckily, it disengaged and resumed circling overhead.

"What the—?" Pax cried, finally waking up.

"It's a bat!" I screamed from under the covers. "It's a vampire bat trying to eat my face!"

"What?! Are you serious?" Pax scrambled to get under his covers.

"Get it, Pax!" I begged. "Get it!"

"Get it?" Pax asked. "No way. I don't do bats. Get it yourself!" He pulled his covers over his head even tighter.

"Come on, Pax! Hit it with your lacrosse stick!"

"Do you have any idea how much that thing cost me? I'm not going to get rabies all over it."

"A lacrosse stick can't get rabies, you dolt!"

"Whatever. I'm just saying that thing is expensive and bat guts would ruin it."

"How are we even related?" I sighed.

Pax didn't reply.

We both lay there hoping the other would take care of the vermin now hanging silently on the drapes. I flipped on my side and peered across the space between our beds. "Pax," I whispered, because I was afraid if I was too loud the bat might feel threatened and attack me.

Pax flipped on his side and faced me. "What?" he whispered back. "Do you have a plan?"

"Yes," I said. "There's a bible in the drawer. Hit the bat with the bible. Smite it!"

"What the heck does smite mean, Plum? Did you get bit? Do you have rabies now?"

"Of course I don't have rabies, Pax! I am trapped in a room with a bat and I need you to get it."

"Are you crazy? Notgunnahappen." He shook his head.

"Come on, Pax. It has to be you."

"Says who?"

"Says society, man. Be a man! Nut up! Just, y'know, man up, get some balls, or whatever. You're the boy," I said. "I'm the girl."

"Nope. You're Ms. Independent. You're Ms. I Can Do Anything You Can Do Better! No one tells Plum she can't do something. So, here you go! Go for it. Go be a bat wrangler. Show me how it's done."

"I can't," I whimpered. "I'm afraid. Don't you see that?"

"Well, news flash, I'm not feeling so brave myself."

"Okay, go get Dad, then," I said.

"Yeah, that's a thousand nopes. I am not moving from this spot," Pax said. "That thing is going to attack."

"One of us has to go for help," I argued. "We can't stay like this all night."

"You are the oldest," Pax reminded me. "You should rescue your *widdle brudah*."

I tried to compromise. "How about we go together?"

"Rock, paper, scissors," Pax said.

"Fine," I agreed.

"Rock, paper, scissors, shoot," we said in unison.

I went rock, because I used logic. Rocks are hard. You can throw rocks. A rock would kill a bat. Pax went paper, because he knows I almost always do rock. Damn me and my predictability!!! "Best out of three," I said.

"Nope." Pax pulled the covers back over his head. His voice was muffled. "Go. Get. Dad."

I was thoroughly outraged. Pax pretends he's all big and strong, but when it really comes time to show what he's got, he turns into a giant pansy! I took a deep breath and peeked at the bat. It still clung to the curtains. That was good. The problem was the curtains were right next to the door. That was bad. I was going to have to get by the bat to open the door. Whyyyyyyyyy did my mother have to pick this joint? Of course a hotel consisting of concrete teepees, a dirt parking lot, and a broken pool would have bats. The Bates Motel would have been a more welcome choice at this point.

I screwed up my courage. "Let's do this," I said like I was an action hero or something. I threw off the blankets, I shoved my feet into my shoes, and ran for the door. (Okay, lumbered is probably a better word since I don't run.) Because I am grace personified, a terrible sequence of events happened next. In my haste to get out of the room quickly, I caught my toe on the corner of a chair, which then made me stumble. I overcorrected, and this resulted in me stepping on my untied shoelaces. This caused me to lose my balance and sent me careening toward the door, my hands flailing wildly to catch something—anything—to break my fall.

They caught something all right.

They caught the curtains where the bat hung. I fell into the curtains and snatched them right off the rod as I tumbled to the ground. The bat was startled (duh!) and naturally went directly for my face. I swatted it away, essentially throwing it onto the top of my head. I sleep with my hair piled up in a loose, messy bun and apparently that hairstyle is like a tar pit for bats, because that flying rodent mired itself in there like it was motherfracking La Brea. I might have lumbered before, but it's amazing how fast I can move when there is a bat lodged in my hair. I jumped up and ran around the room in circles crying hysterically.

"IT'S IN MY HAIR!!!" I screamed. "PAX!!!! HELP ME, YOU ASSHOLE!"

"Get outside, get outside!" Pax screamed. He threw open the door and shoved me outside into the night and slammed the door behind me.

"Pax!" I screamed, banging on the door. I felt the bat move and I swatted at it frantically, causing myself to fall down again (shocker). I could feel the bat digging its tiny feet into my scalp, trying to extricate itself from my trap. "BURN IT WITH FIRE!!!" I screamed. "Help!"

Lights in the surrounding teepees turned on and sleepy travelers exited to investigate the noise.

I heard Dad say, "What's going on? Pax? Plum? Are you okay?"

At the sound of Dad's voice, my brave brother Pax opened the door a crack. "Dad! Plum! Bat! Hair! Kill!" Pax yelled. He slammed the door shut again. He was an absolute mess. Even though I was wrestling with a bat, I made a mental note that when the zombie apocalypse happens, I must leave Pax behind. He is obviously worthless in an emergency—plus he eats a crap ton.

"Plum!" Mom rushed to my side.

"There's a bat in my hair, Mommy!" Yeah, I called her Mommy. Let's see how brave you'd be if there was a bat setting up shop in your hair.

"Oh my God!" Mom actually took a step back. Let me repeat that. Mom took a *step back*! You know how your mom is always like, "I'd do anything for you, pumpkin. I'd jump in front of a bus or take a bullet for you"? They're lying—or buses and bullets are fine, but bats are deal-breakers, I'm not sure.

"Mom! Don't leave me!" I screamed, reaching for her.

"Look out!" It was the manager of the motel. He ran over with a butterfly net and smacked it down on my head. Quite hard, actually. "Ow!" I said.

He said, "Easy there. Be still. Don't be afraid."

"I'm trying," I whispered.

"Oh, um, okay, great. 'Cause, actually, I was talking to the bat."

THE BAT???!!! Had everyone lost their minds?? My brother was a wuss, my mom abandoned me, and now this guy was comforting the bat that had assaulted his guest! I was like, *I'm going to murder this place on Yelp.*

The manager wiggled his fingers through my hair. "They're very gentle creatures," he said. "And they're vital to the ecosystem. She's more afraid than you are right now."

I'd nearly peed my pants. There was no way that stupid bat was more afraid than me.

He wiggled some more and finally I felt the bat break free. "There you go, sweetheart," he said. This time I didn't bother trying to reply, because I knew it was the bat he was speaking to. "I got you. You're okay."

I rolled away from the weirdo manager and his new girlfriend, Batricia. What? I felt like we'd spent enough time together at that point I'd earned the right to name her.

"Plum!" Mom started to come to me and I held up a finger to stop her.

"No, you don't get to touch me. No, no, no," I said, wagging my finger. "You had your chance. You blew it. Blew. It. I want to leave this place. *Now.*"

Before the sun was up we were gone. I am writing this in my room at a 3-star hotel with non-vibrating beds, Wi-Fi, a real pool, and room service.

Plum's Punch List:

1. Really? You have to ask? BATS!!!!!!

Thursday

August 11

Today was "Buy All the Things for the New House Day" and our new minivan was so full there was barely a spot for me. Even though Olga and Igor are on their way with a full truck, Mom thinks we need more stuff. The new house is bigger than the one in New Jersey, and Mom doesn't think she has have enough crap to fill it. So for the last few days all we've done is drive around town buying accent rugs and curtains and lamps. She keeps asking my opinion. Like I care. Do people really have such strong feelings about lamps? They all looked the same to me. As long as they turn on and off, what does it matter? They're lamps!

"But Plum, this one is matte black and this one is glossy black," Mom said.

I wanted to say, "For cripes' sake, woman, just pick a freaking black lamp already!" We'd had so much together time that I was ready to explode.

"Now that I think about it," she said. "I really like the look of the ones with the glass bases. What do you think? Do you like the clear or frosted glass, Plum?"

ARGGGGGGGHHHHHHH!!!!!!

Dad was pretty quiet until it was time to order a sofa. He didn't give a fig about lamps, but *Lawd* he could wax on for days about sofas. Who knew that was his thing? I think he sat on every single sofa in the place. Probably 200 sofas. No joke. He was like motherhumping Goldilocks. "Too firm. Too soft. Too high. Too deep. Too scratchy. Too ugly. Too pretty. Too bumpy. Too feathery. Too corduroy-y."

Yes, "corduroy-y" was something he actually said. That was when the saleswoman who right up until that moment had been nothing but perky and helpful looked like she wanted to beat Dad over the head with one of Mom's new frosted glass lamps. She wisely excused herself to answer an imaginary phone call before she did something foolish that would cost her a large sale and possibly her career.

Mom disregarded Dad completely and ordered the corduroy-y couch and a hideous leather recliner he had deemed "perfect."

"That chair is awful, but marriage is a compromise," Mom lectured me and Pax as she handed over her credit card to the once-again-perky saleswoman. "We'll stick it in the basement or something."

Mom was thrilled with her new lamps (she changed to matte black at the last minute), couch, and dining room table, but the thing she was most excited about was ordering furniture for my room.

"I don't need new furniture," I told her. I have a wrought iron daybed that had been hers when she was a teenager. It was rickety and a bit squeaky every time I turned over, but I loved it. Maybe it's weird, but it makes me happy to know that goofy teenage Mom slept in the same bed as me. That she cried about boys and laughed with her friends there too. It sounds crazy, but the bed makes me feel closer to Mom. I also had a dresser Mom found at a neighbor's garage sale a few years ago. We wrestled it home in my wagon and painted it a bright fire-engine red. It was really bright at first, so I took a black Sharpie and started drawing designs on it. Now it's covered in my artwork and graffiti. I started drawing on it when I was nine, so it's a bit of a mess. You can see when I was obsessed with puppy dogs and then weird doll faces and finally I graduated to bizarre eyeballs. I must admit, the eyeballs are kind of freaky. I'm glad that stage didn't last very long. The dresser wasn't in great shape when we got it, and it's been deteriorating ever since. Mom was itching to get rid of it.

"Plum, wouldn't you like some new grown-up things for your room? My old daybed was supposed to be temporary, and that dresser of yours is falling apart. We've spent more on duct tape to keep it together than it's actually worth. I was thinking we could do your room in bright pink with black and white accents," she said. "Maybe a loft-style bed and a zebra-print couch tucked underneath?"

"I like black and white," I said carefully. "But I'm not sure about pink…or the zebra print." I was trying to be nice, but I wanted to scream, "It's like you don't even know me, woman!" Why was she starting in with this pink nonsense? Where was it coming from? What had I done in my entire life to make her think I'd ever want a pink room and a zebra-print couch? I mean, sure, I have pink hair, but that's hair, not a wall. I don't wear pink clothing of any kind. I haven't since she stopped dressing me and even then I didn't like pink, I just wore it because I was too little to resist being dressed by her.

"Let's just try it," she said, practically begging me. "When I was your age I always wanted a pink room and my parents couldn't afford to do it."

Now do you see? There it was. Usually Mom is pretty cool, but then there are times where she wants to live vicariously through me. I bet, if I'd pushed her, I would have discovered that when she was a girl, she also wanted a zebra-print couch in her room.

Pax is lucky, he never has to deal with this kind of nonsense. Mom doesn't try to live vicariously through him, and Dad definitely does not. That's because Dad never wanted anything as a child. Or at least that's what he tells us. Truthfully, I don't think Dad was ever a kid. What kid doesn't want *anything*? Don't get me wrong, I don't want a zebra-print couch, but there are a bunch of things I *do* want. Dad swears he was happy to wear the no-name tennis shoes Grammy bought at the grocery store. "The extra 'd' in Addidas made them faster." He says he enjoyed wearing his brother's hand-me-down clothes. "*Hello*, vintage has always been a hot look." And he constantly assures us he was absolutely thrilled to play with the sticks he found on the ground instead of silly, boring store-bought toys. "You can't imagine all the things you can do with sticks," Dad said.

He was right. I can't imagine it. Not at all.

"Can we at least wait so I can see what my room looks like?" I asked.

"Maybe a couch won't even fit in there."

Mom looked disappointed. "I guess so. But it will. I measured," she said softly. "Twice."

Plum's Punch List:

1. Lamps—matte or shiny or glass ones
2. Fugly leather chairs
3. Zebra-print couches
4. Compromise

Friday

August 12

Olga and Igor finally arrived! I was so excited to see a familiar face that I actually ran out to meet the truck.

"Ack, so flat here," Igor said as he jumped down from the cab of the moving truck.

"Hot too," Olga added. "You like it, Plum?"

I shrugged. "Not really, but what choice do I have?"

Igor frowned. "I leaved Ukraine when I was fifteen."

Olga nodded. "You old enough to be alone, Plum."

I wasn't sure what to say, so I just said. "We'd better get to work before Mom has a cow. She's got a whole plan drawn up for where she wants everything."

"Good," Olga said. "Make my job easier. Let's go, Igor."

Mom's plan did make the unloading go much faster. Olga and Igor were done by late afternoon. Olga found me to say goodbye. "Last chance, Plum," she said.

"Last chance?"

"Igor and I are leaving. We drive to New Jersey tonight. Want ride? We drop you somewhere along the way?"

"Nah, I'm good, Olga. It's not so bad here."

Olga looked around and shuddered. "If you say so."

Jesus. Olga can be so serious! It's not like I was starving to death or being threatened with prison or anything. I was just being forced to change schools and live in a greige community.

My new house is cooler than I thought it would be. I knew it was bigger than the house in Jersey, but I didn't know it would be so big. Mom and Dad have a giant bedroom on the first floor. Our Realtor, Penny, called it a "luxurious master suite." I called it sick.

Pax and I have our own luxurious/sick suites upstairs. My walk-in closet is as big as my whole bedroom was in Jersey. I also got my own bathroom. No more sharing with Pax. Hallelujah! That boy's morning regimen is longer than a Kardashian's. Not to mention that the cloud of Axe body spray he leaves behind is dangerous to my health.

Mom and I compromised on our visions for my room. Three walls are hot pink and the fourth wall is black, but it's chalkboard paint, so I can draw on it. I kept her daybed but got new bedding for it: black and white with zebra-print throw pillows that I can chuck in the closet as soon as I get sick of them. I also got a new dresser and a desk. I actually like the way my room turned out. The pink is kind of cool, but I'll never tell Mom.

There's a bonus room between my room and Pax's room that Mom said can be our hangout space. It has a refrigerator and a microwave and it's where Mom put a giant TV, our game consoles, and an enormous sofa pit. I might never leave the house again.

Mom and Dad have been working overtime to sell Kansas and I must admit, I'm warming up. The fully stocked mini-fridge is helping, but I still want a beanbag chair.

"I can't imagine a better place to curl up and read a good book, Mom." (When your mother is a professional writer, she will do anything to encourage reading and/or writing. This is how I get the bulk of the cool things I want: wireless cat-ear headphones are totally helpful for reading or listening to audiobooks; a mermaid-tail blanket is the best way to keep warm while reading; fancy gel pens inspire epic journal entries, etc., etc. I could do this all day.) But then she looked at how much beanbag chairs cost. Did you know that beanbag chairs are stupid expensive? Yeah, me neither.

"Sorry, Plum," she said. "I've got to stick to my budget, and I've spent everything I'm spending on you."

That's when I rubbed my head and said, "Ow, my head still hurts a little from where that bat attacked me. Remember when the bat was caught in my hair and you didn't help me, Mommy?"

"Nice try, Plum, but you can't keep playing the bat card on me," she said. "You already got a new pair of Converse this week when you claimed your others were ruined in the bat onslaught. I refuse to be guilt-tripped by you any longer."

Whatevs, I won't be deterred. Maybe I'll call Grandma and tell her about Batricia's vicious attack on me. If nothing else, she'd probably buy me the beanbag chair out of pity and to make Mom mad.

Realtor Penny swore our street is full of kids, but I haven't seen one yet. Wait. That's not true. I have seen a few minivans drive by loaded with kids dressed in various uniforms indicating their extracurricular activity preferences. Everything from soccer to ballet to swim team, but I haven't seen any of these well-dressed kids actually set foot outside. The giant garage doors on their McMansions go up, the minivans (or the occasional SUV) whip out and then sail past our front yard. The drivers are never the same person, but they're always the same type of person: a mom with stick-straight blond hair hanging in sheets down past her shoulders, giant black sunglasses covering the upper half of her face and a Starbucks cup covering the lower half, the green straw clenched between her recently whitened teeth so she can easily suck down her soy pumpkin carrot chai decaf tea latte with nonfat whip or whatever disgusting swill the moms are guzzling these days. When they come back from basket-weaving class or batting practice or wherever they've been, the mom hits the magic garage door button from the corner and never touches her brakes until they're safely ensconced in their perfectly arranged garage and the giant door is already closing behind them. Sometimes I wait to see if anyone will come outside. Very rarely a mom will go to check the mail. She's usually dressed for yoga, but I get the distinct impression those yoga pants she's wearing have never been to yoga. I always hope the kids will come outside, but they never do. It's weird, because I can see bikes and skateboards hanging neatly on hooks or placed on shelves on the walls of those garages. I've glimpsed basketballs and soccer balls piled carefully in tubs, so I know they've got outdoor equipment. Whether it gets used or not is a mystery. I have decided the kids in Kansas must be allergic to the sun or something.

Don't get me wrong, it's not like I'm some kind of Janie Jock over here, but I have been known to ride my bike a block or two or throw around a ball with Pax. In New Jersey we had a tree house in the backyard. Even though I outgrew playing in it, I still liked to go up there a lot of days and spend some time reading or drawing. I was outside, but I wasn't working up a sweat or anything, but that still counts as being outside.

Mom says not to worry. That school will start soon and I'll meet a bunch of kids then. She says I'll find all kinds of new friends. Is she talking about me? Plum Parrish? The girl who had a hard time making friends with the group of kids she'd known since preschool? Does Mom just think I will saunter into my new high school and immediately be welcomed by everyone? I can't tell if Mom is an eternal optimist or losing her mind.

Plum's Punch List:

1. Over-scheduled kids

Saturday

August 13

I couldn't sleep last night. The new house is noisy, but also too quiet. Does that make sense? The noises are different than what I'm used to. My house in New Jersey was on a busy road so I always heard the traffic, no matter what time of night. Here it's silent, except it's not. The bugs won't shut up. They chirp and click all night long. And I swear I heard a wolf howling at the moon or a bear growling outside my window. Dad says that's impossible, but I'm not buying it. I know what I heard. I think. Or maybe I dreamed that part during the one hour I actually slept. Either way, it was *loud*.

I couldn't sleep, so I tossed and turned for a bit, praying all the critters would quiet down, and just when I was getting to used to all the noises and they weren't bothering me too much anymore and I was drifting off to sleep…my brain was like, "Hello? (tap, tap, tap) Is this thing on?"

UGH. WHHHHHHHHYYYYYYYY, Brain?

My brain was like, "Hi, let's chat, Plum. You know you suck, right? I just wanted to make sure that you got the message. You know that you're going to get to your new school and everyone will hate your guts because, did I mention yet how much you suck? Yeah. You're going to fail because you probably didn't learn the same things in eighth grade that the kids in Kansas learned. You will flunk out of ninth grade and you'll be forced to live with your parents for the rest of your life. I hope you like this room, because it will be yours forever. And then when your parents die, *MAYBE* Pax will let you live in his garage. No promises, though, because as I said before, you suck. Like, donkey balls suck. That's how much you suck. Oh, and your face is dumb, too. Just saying."

The thing is, once my brain starts insulting me, there's no stopping it. There was no way I could go back to sleep. I laid there in the dark for a while listening to my brain tell me what a loser I was, until I finally remembered Mom's overused dorky expression, "You do you, Plum. You do you."

It might be dorky, but it worked, because all of a sudden I was like, *Yeah, Brain!! I do me!* I started thinking about what Pax said about reinventing myself. I needed to figure out some ways to suck less, I guess. I'd already started with the hair, but maybe I needed to take it a step further. But I didn't have a clue where to begin. What did I know about being cool or accepted? Frankly, not a lot. But I'm not dumb. I can learn new things, so I decided to treat it like a research paper.

Last year I had to do a research paper on Queen Elizabeth I. At first I thought she was the queen who lives in England right now. WRONG! She lived almost 500 years ago and she's super famous. I didn't know that until I went online and found a bunch of articles and stories about her.

I figured that's what I needed to do again, only my topic was: how not to suck. I was sure there were tons of ideas and advice out there about making yourself over. How to fit in, make friends, and conquer the world!

So, I got out of bed, grabbed my laptop, and got started.

The first search brought up a jaunty, bright blog with a peppy-sounding list: I'm Popular and You Can Be Too! 100 Ways to Be Popular in High School!

Barf. This was going to be harder than I expected, I thought.

The list was written by some girl who swears she's THE MOST popular girl in her high school. Side note, I don't know how she can find time to be popular when she's writing 100 ways to be popular. I would think that would take precious time away from her social life. Anyhoo, I kept going. But then I had this little nagging thought that wouldn't go away. What were her motives for making such a list? Why would she do this? Was she getting extra credit at school, or did this count toward her community service requirements? She said she wrote this list to help the "less fortunate overcome there terrible social stature." Look, I might have a terrible social stature, but my spelling is impeccable. I wanted to send her a dictionary so she could learn the difference between *their*, *there*, and *they're*. After a few more futile online searches, I decided to take my chances with Ms. Popular since she didn't purport to be a grammarian, only an expert on popularity. I could overlook her misspellings and focus on her advice, since all the other sites I found appeared to be written by middle-aged dudes with "doctor" in front of their names. *Snooze.*

1. Have an amazing appearance.

"Oh come on! Are you kidding me?" I griped and I almost threw my laptop across the room when I read that one. I mean, seriously! *Of course* popular people look good. That's why they're popular!! No one elects Pizza Face to be homecoming king. Even though I was pissed off, I decided to keep reading. After all, this was a list claiming to include 100 pieces of advice, surely there were some nuggets of wisdom tucked in there somewhere between "be pretty" and "be popular."

2. Maintain amazing hair. Change the style often: straight, curly, up, or down. Have fun with your hair!

"Okay! Now we're talking," I said. I was like, *Psht, I have amazing hair already! Done and done.* I could mark that one off my list. I scanned her list for more things I could mark off immediately. Marking things off lists is kind of my thing. I feel a great sense of accomplishment even though I haven't actually *done* anything. I quickly eliminated: "maintain clean nails, shave your legs and pits, brush your teeth." Seriously? Are there high schoolers who aren't brushing their teeth? Is this a real-life problem? If the criteria to be popular is brush your teeth and clean your fingernails, then maybe I'm more popular than I thought. I looked for some things I wasn't already doing but would take minimal effort and raise my popular quotient. I found one:

12. Get an amazing backpack.

I know, what is the deal with the word "amazing" and this girl, right? I need to get her a thesaurus to go with her dictionary. But this is good advice. I've been using the same backpack since fifth grade. There's nothing wrong with it. It's not like it's got My Little Pony on it or something, but it's just sort of blah. It's not amazing. I can get a new one.

There were some more suggestions that required shopping: I'm going to need new shoes, some "amazing" accessories, and a "signature scent." I have no idea what a signature scent is, but supposedly all popular girls have one. I'll see what I can find.

Finally, near the middle of the list she moved on to what I like to call "the behavior modification zone." Basically, it boils down to: there are only so many body parts you can shave, tweeze, and pluck and only so many amazing things you can buy, but if you don't have the right attitude and the right outlook, then you're NOTHING.

26. Be yourself, but be pleasant. No one likes unpleasant people.
27. Be positive. No one likes a grump!

Well, fudge. I'm screwed, right? Pleasant and positive??? I can't even imagine what a day full of positivity would look like. I can't live my life like I'm surrounded by rainbows and baby seals everywhere I go. My grumpiness is part of my charm! Screw her. My irritation and anger keeps me warm at night and lets me know I'm still alive.

28. Be funny, but not too funny. Sometimes funny people make others feel stupid.

No, no, no. This one's an absolute deal-breaker. I can't help if it people are too dumb to get my humor. Sarcasm is my love language and if it makes people feel uncomfortable and dumb, then I'm doing it right.

And then there was this gem:

60. Show off your talents. Everyone is good at something, and everyone wants to see you strut your stuff.

No, we don't. STAHP. I would argue there are too many people in this world strutting their stuff and it's stuff that has no business being strutted. I blame our parents. They clapped like monkeys and gave us treats for doing idiotic things like hanging up our coats properly. We were never told "no" and were always treated like special snowflakes. I don't give a shit that Johnny Halfwit can kick a ball farther than anyone else; he does not need to document that on YouTube so we can all fall over ourselves to congratulate him.

79. Hang around the popular cliques and be helpful to them. Even if they won't let you join, they'll notice you and give you small tasks to do on their behalf. Then others will think you're popular by proximity.

"Is this chick for real?" I shrieked, because was someone really going to think that because I'm carrying Ms. Popular's *ah-may-zing* backpack, then I must be popular too? My self-esteem is pretty jacked up, but not that jacked up. There's no way I'd ever be anyone's bitch hoping that was the road to popularity.

Just when I thought Ms. Popular's advice couldn't get any worse, she went off the rails completely:

92. Don't just limit your popularity to school. Be popular EVERYWHERE! School, church, teams, camp, etc.

Oh?! Was that all I had to do? Just be popular EVERYWHERE??? Is my sarcasm font working? Are you kidding me? Like it's just that easy. Like I can just snap my fingers and suddenly I'm popular everywhere. I can't even be popular in my own house! It's going to be hard enough to try and make the cut in a brand-new high school, and now I'm supposed to be thinking about how I can be the queen of Cabin 10 at Camp Happy Days, too?

Gee, thanks, Ms. Popular! Great advice! Bravo!

In case I was confused by all her sage pieces of advice, I should have just jumped straight to number 100. Because number 100 cleared it all up for me. Ms. Popular saved her best piece of advice for the end:

100. Be cool.

Ya think?? Of course! How silly of me! All these years I've forgotten to be cool!! Thank you, thank you, thank you!

Ugh. Oh my God, that list sucked so hard I felt worse after I read it than I did before I started! I'm never going to be popular and honestly, if that's what it takes, I don't want to be. Her advice is awful!!! ARGH!!!!!!!

Heyyy, I'm back. I might have overreacted a bit earlier. I've been thinking, and what can I say? Desperate times call for desperate measures. There might be a few good takeaways I could implement. For instance, I've already got great hair, I like shopping, so I can keep an eye out for a new amazing backpack, maybe some interesting clothes, and I could work on a slight—very slight—change in attitude. But that's it, there's nothing else of any value on that list. Definitely no signature scents, unless I can count flop sweat as mine.

Plum's Punch List:

1. Popular girls who think they can make you popular too
2. Signature scents

Tuesday

August 16

Sunset Pines High School. SPHS.

That's the name of my new school. It's smaller than my old school, but also kind of bigger. It's sprawly—my old school was three floors. SPHS is all one floor. Kind of half a wagon wheel with spokes shooting off. It's got a lot of land around it. The strangest part is that "pines" is in the name, but there is literally not one tree on the school grounds. It's all grass. There's a section off to the side with a giant sign announcing: NO MOWING! NATIVE PRAIRIE GRASS AREA. I've never seen native prairie grass, but to me it just looked a lot like a field of three-foot-tall weeds. What I'm saying is, if those native prairie grasses were growing in my yard, Mom would have made me pull them. I can see where they got the sunset part from. You can't miss the sunsets in Kansas. Every night there it is, bolder and, if I'm honest, more beautiful than the night before. But pines?? Where are the pines? Maybe the school should be called Sunset Weeds High School.

We went to new student orientation tonight. Well, really, just Mom and I went. Pax didn't want to go. He said he had no desire to be shown around the school by "some principal's pet bootlicker" (his words, not mine). He said they weren't going to show him anything he couldn't find on his own: the cafeteria, the gym, the boys' bathroom. He says he'd rather "acquire his first flavor of SPHS" (again, his words, not mine) on the first day of school.

And Dad didn't go because he had to work late—again. This new job sucks, BTW. Dad is never around anymore and when he is he's so fricking CRABBY!

Mom said Pax could stay home, but she thought it was important I go. "Maybe you'll like the bootlicker who gives us a tour and she can be your new BFF?" she suggested.

I was not convinced.

"We can stop for ice cream on the way home," she promised.

She had me at ice cream. You have no idea. I'm always so bored it doesn't take much to bribe me to go anywhere, but food always helps get me off the couch. Shoot, I probably would have gone if she'd just offered a lollipop, so of course I put on real pants for ice cream.

We got to SPHS about ten minutes after the orientation started. A few lost-looking parents and students were milling around the gym. They moved back and forth between two tables. One table was manned by three moms with the biggest smiles, eyes, and hair I've ever seen. They were foisting entire boxes of homemade cookies on anyone who got within five feet of their table. "Sugar cookie? We've also got nut-free, gluten-free, sugar-free, egg-free, dairy-free cookies. Take one—or a bunch!" It looked like they had been expecting a lot more people than actually showed up.

The second table had one bored man sitting behind it, playing idly on his phone. He had stacks of flyers for Band, Spanish Club, Mathletes, and Debate Club. He didn't even acknowledge the few people who stopped by his table to pick up a flyer or two.

Mom went to the flyer table first. "Oooh, Mathletes," she said, picking up a bright yellow paper.

The man didn't lift his head. "Girl or boy?" he asked, never taking his eyes off his phone.

What difference does that make? I wanted to shout. But I didn't, because I'm trying to be more positive now. Even though that online popularity list sucked, there were a few more tidbits I had gleaned after some pondering and even Mom says what you put out in the world is what you get back. So, I'm beginning to think that *maybe* I've been putting out a little too much negativity and that's why I'm so angry…and a lot to handle…and weird. And so, I have decided I must work at being more positive.

So, here was me being positive: I was *positive* that guy was a dolt.

Meh. Close enough. At least I didn't say it out loud. Baby steps.

I could tell Mom was also surprised by the man's behavior. Her eyes flashed, but she immediately took a deep breath (she, too, has been working on the energy she's putting out into the universe). "Boy," she said, and I wasn't even the slightest bit offended. I know my strengths—well, actually, I'm still trying to figure out my strengths, but math has been ruled out completely.

The man sucked on his teeth, obviously disappointed. "Too bad. We could use a girl. They're rare in Mathletics—they're the unicorns. Know what I mean? Kind of throws the other teams off their game when you've got a girl competing." He sighed sadly. "Is he in sports?"

"Yes," Mom said.

The man snorted and his eyes went back to his phone. "Yeah, probably not a good fit, then."

"What is that supposed to mean?" Mom demanded. She was getting mad. She'd quit taking deep breaths and her neck was getting splotchy. That happens when she's super pissed off and she's trying to hold it together.

The man sighed loudly and put down his phone. He raised his head and finally looked straight at Mom. "I've been the coach of the Chess, Mathletics, and Robotics teams for five years now. In my experience, the kids who play sports rarely make the time that is necessary to succeed on my teams. These are not your typical after-school programs. These are serious organizations, not a babysitting service. I'm not here for my health. I'm here to win. I'm here to get these kids to the tops of their games and if their head is out in la-la land thinking about the soccer goal they made or the home run they scored over the weekend, then they're not here—" he rapped the table loudly "—doing the work that's necessary to win." He picked up his phone and went back to crushing candy. "Thus, I prefer not to work with kids who are in sports."

I wanted to yell, *Umm … news flash, dummy: your "very serious organization" is a total joke. That's why no one is at your table. People would rather gag down gluten-free cookies than interrupt your scintillating candy matching game. Because nobody takes Chess Club seriously.*

My mom is not a tall person, but she raised herself up as high as she could and she puffed out her chest. I've seen that move enough times to know what was coming. *Uh-oh, Candy Man,* I thought. *Now you're gonna get it.*

Mom unleashed on him. "You may *prefer* not to work with athletic, well-rounded children, but the last time I checked, anyone can sign up for these teams. There is no skill level requirement or even an attendance requirement. My children are new to this school and I am trying to find them something to do that will broaden their minds and introduce them to new friends. I am looking for something that they might enjoy, but still be educational. I thought maybe you were sitting at this table to advertise such offerings, but apparently you are nothing but a doorstop. Thank you for your time. You've been absolutely worthless. Let's go, Plum." Mom dropped the flyer on the table and turned her back on the man.

Mr. Candy Crush's mouth flapped just like I imagined Mr. Bubbles's did when he was dying on my floor.

Mom muttered curses under her breath when we pulled up to the cookie table. I couldn't make out much, but I did hear "jackwagon" and "punk nugget," which I will immediately be adding to my repertoire of alternative swear words.

"Well, hi there!" the lady with the biggest hair of the three said. "Welcome to Sunset Pines!" And then she roared at us. Like seriously roared. Like, *RAWR!*

Mom and I must have looked utterly confused because Big Hair Number Two said, "It's okay. She's not crazy! You're new, right?"

I nodded.

Big Hair Number Two continued, "Well, welcome! We're the Sunset Pines Pumas. *Rawr!* You're a Puma now, sweetie!"

Plum the Puma? Of course I am. I ask you, could Kansas be any worse?

At my old school we were the North Stars. I liked being a North Star.

I had not thought about what our mascot in Kansas would be. I guess puma wasn't so bad when you think of the alternatives. It could have been the Sunset Pines High School Farmers, or SPHS Cows, or SPHS Pioneers Who Survived Dysentery.

"Rawr!" Mom said, batting her hand like a paw.

"Ohh, I love that!" Big Hair One said and batted back at Mom. Pretty soon they were having a little kitty fight thing going on while Big Hair Two cheered them on.

OMG, Mom. Staaaaaahp!

Big Hair Two stopped swatting at Mom and asked, "Tell me, Mom, are you thinking of joining the PTA?"

"What?" Mom was flustered. You see, the PTA has always been a weird thing with Mom. She works from home and has a fairly flexible schedule and so the PTA moms love her because they think she can drop everything and go to the school to sell T-shirts at noon. Mom gets all pissy, because she feels like yes, her schedule is flexible, but she should be treated like all the other working moms with a traditional job. She can't just abandon her work to do the PTA's work. Mom feels like the PTA moms don't respect her job the way they would respect someone who works in a cubicle farm. Because of this, Mom hasn't volunteered at our school since Pax and I were in kindergarten. But then, she's overwhelmed with Mommy Guilt when she sees all the desperate pleas for chaperones and committee heads and stuff, and so then she feels like she's letting me and Pax down when she ignores them. And also, you can't forget she feels judged by all the other moms. The ones who are stuck in a cubicle farm are like, "Oh, it must be so nice to have the flexibility. I'd looooove to work at the school." And the stay-at-home moms are like, "You don't even have a boss. You could totally come and help us; you just don't want to." Meanwhile, no one has ever said any of these things to Mom, but she tells us she's very intuitive and so she can feel what they're thinking. In case you haven't guessed yet, Mom is a one-woman freak show.

"Oh, I'm sorry, but I can't. But I'd be happy to write a check for anything you might need," Mom said.

Big Hair One plastered a fake smile on her face and said, "Well, what we really need are volunteers. We've got plenty of revenue streams, but not enough bodies to fill the roles. We're always seeking out women who are looking for something to get them out of the house and into leadership roles."

"It's also great for resume-building. For when you want to go back to work," said Big Hair Two.

Mom smiled. "Well, I already work, so…"

"I see," said Big Hair One, slightly offended. She was probably intuitive as well and could feel Mom judging her.

I noticed Big Hair Three hadn't said anything to us. She just watched my mother with a cold and calculating eye. I knew what she was doing. I've seen that look before. She was trying to figure out how she knew Mom. And then the light bulb went on. *Ding!* "Are you Lacy Drawers?" Big Hair Three asked, kind of rudely, actually. It was more of an accusation than a question.

Uh-oh, I thought.

My mother went still. I wasn't sure what she'd do. Her real name isn't Lacy Drawers, of course. It's Lily Parrish. But, at the same time, she IS Lacy Drawers. Mom's work-at-home job title is writer and her pen name is Lacy Drawers. Mom writes romance. Which isn't a big deal, except she writes novels that are meant for adults. The sexy kind—erotica. You know, those ones with the half-naked couples kissing on the covers? Only hers are strange; they're humorous erotic. Who wants to laugh during sex? I don't know. I guess people like it. I wouldn't know. I'm not allowed to read what she writes—ever. Well, maybe when I'm in college or something. Mom hasn't given me an actual date, but really I'm okay with it. I'm more of a dystopian kind of girl anyway. I think romance is overrated and obnoxious. Who wants to be around such happy yet troubled people? There's always so much drama that comes with love. They can never just be happy, there's always another guy who loves the girl too or her parents want to break them up. It's just annoying. Nope. I'd rather read a nice depressing story about the world ending. Sometimes Mom admits she's Lacy Drawers and sometimes she doesn't. Dad, Pax, and I have learned to keep our mouths shut and let Mom take the lead whenever this question comes up.

"Are you a fan of Lacy's work?" Mom asked Big Hair Three.

Big Hair Three narrowed her eyes. "No. I think her work is deplorable.

There is absolutely no merit to it. It's immoral and disgusting and should be banned completely."

Mom smirked. "I see. Well, then nice to meet you. I'm Lacy Drawers."

BOOM! Can you believe she said that? Sometimes my mom is kind of a badass. She really doesn't care what people think of her. In fact, I think she actually enjoys poking the haters. I could never be like that.

Mom stuck out her hand, but Big Hair Three ignored it completely! Ohemgee, it was so awkward. Mom just stared her down, smiling as big as she could while Big Hair Three sneered at her. Only because I know Mom so well, I knew she was a little uncomfortable, but she refused to back down. I, personally, wanted to die. Sure it was a badass move at first, but at that point it was getting uncomfortable. Why didn't she just slink away like a normal person? Why did she have to make it into *A Thing*?

Big Hairs One and Two were perplexed. They weren't sure what to do, so they stood there looking back and forth between Mom and Big Hair Three like they were at a tennis match.

"I knew it!" Big Hair Three said. "As soon as you walked in the door, I knew it was you."

"You recognized me?" Mom asked, putting her hand down (finally!).

"Of course! I've been to your website a number of times. I've read your books and I listened to a podcast that featured you."

"Wow, for someone who hates what I do, you sure do know a lot about me," Mom said, popping a nut-free, gluten-free, sugar-free, dairy-free, egg-free cookie in her mouth. "Blech," she said. She immediately spit it out in a napkin and used another napkin to wipe off her tongue.

"They're healthy," Big Hair One squeaked.

"They should be illegal," Mom replied.

If Big Hairs One and Two had been wearing pearls, they would have clutched them.

It was right about then I started wishing for a giant hole to appear in the floor. I would have gladly fallen down a bottomless crater at that point. Anything to get away. I am soooo not built for confrontation.

"It's *my job* to know about you," Big Hair Three said. "I head up the

Banned Books Committee at the county library. It's not a paid position or anything. I *volunteer* my time to rid the shelves of filth before it infects our children. I know all about you and your...*ilk*." Big Hair Three wrinkled her nose like my mother smelled bad.

Mom shrugged. "I'm sorry you don't like what I do, but there's no need to be so rude."

"You're a *mother*," Big Hair Three sneered. "What possessed you to write such trash for a living?"

I was stunned. *Trash?* I bristled. My mother doesn't write trash! I know what Mom writes isn't for everyone, but I've never seen anyone take her to task the way Big Hair Three did. I've seen women literally *cry* when they meet Mom. She saves marriages and makes women happier! Apparently you can be forty and still be a mean girl.

"You're right, I *am* a mother and I would appreciate it you'd be respectful in front of my daughter, Plum," Mom said in her best soft-but-deadly voice. "Whatever you think of my writing is your own opinion, but we don't care to hear it. I'm not here tonight as Lacy Drawers. So, let's try again, shall we? Hello, I'm Lily Parrish and this is my daughter, Plum. She's a new incoming freshman." She reached out her hand and Big Hair Three STILL wouldn't shake it! Can you believe it?! I could tell Mom couldn't believe it either. She was angry and kind of embarrassed and she tried to make it light by cracking a joke. She does this a lot. She thinks that humor can defuse tense situations. I disagree with Mom completely on this theory. "What did the shoes say to the pants?" Mom asked.

The Big Hairs stared at her, flabbergasted.

"Sup, britches!"

Where was the dang bottomless crater I'd been praying for? All I could think was, *Please someone kill me.*

Luckily right that moment was when the principal, Mr. Cutler, came over to see if we wanted to join the next tour.

"God, yes!" I practically yelled.

"See ya, britches," Mom said, waving to the Big Hairs.

Jesus. Why was I her daughter?

I followed Mr. Cutler over to a group of parents and students where he introduced us to Emberleigh Davidson.

No, I didn't spell her name wrong. That's really how she spells it. It was written on her name tag in perfect, neat block letters with an adorable heart over the "i." I couldn't look at Mom because I'd start laughing, but I saw her take out her ever-present notebook and make a quick note. My mom collects "terrible" names for characters in her books. The more made up or poorly spelled, the better. Her all-time best-selling series revolves around a couple named Aighmee and Jaysun and Mom gives most of the credit of the books' success to their terrible names. "It's impossible for a reader to forget a story with those two names," she once told me.

Look, I get it. Mom and I are the last people who should get to make fun of someone's name. She named me after a fruit, for goodness' sake. But I'm not really named after a fruit. I'm named after Dad's great-aunt Plumeria. Thank God they dropped the "eria" and just went with Plum. And Pax means peace. Pax was going to be Peter or Parker (Dad's a bit of a *Spider-Man* nut), but when we were newborns the nurses put us in an incubator together and I was always crying and freaking out and he'd reach his tiny baby hand over and touch me and I'd settle right down. "Look, he's a peacemaker," Mom said.

So, Plum and Pax.

NOT WEIRD AT ALL.

Not like Emberleigh.

How did her parents even come up with that name? I don't even get it. It's completely made up, and it's as if they tried to be as complicated as possible with the spelling.

I know I shouldn't, but I couldn't help myself. I already disliked Emberleigh as soon as I met her. I mean, come on. Between her jacked-up name, her perfect penmanship, the precious "i," her sporty-yet-casual-yet-adorable ensemble, and the way she twirled her beautiful hair (that probably took a crap ton of effort to look so effortless), I couldn't find one thing I had in common with her. She looked like someone whose family had an impeccable portrait of themselves dressed alike in a sea of one million sunflowers hanging over the mantle in their living room. I know I shouldn't pre-judge people like that, but I'm rarely wrong, and I've wasted so much of my life trying to find common ground with perfect lemmings like Emberleigh that I refuse to do that anymore.

But then I remembered the popular list:

18. Be friendly. You never know who you'll meet!

Fine, I thought. *I'll try out this "be friendly" thing. Ugh!*

"Hi," I said. "I'm Plum." Now, I might have said it very softly, but I'm almost positive Emberleigh heard me. In case she didn't, I tried again. "Hello, I'm new. My name is Plum Parrish."

I know Emberleigh heard me that time. She didn't speak, but she looked me up and down like I was something she'd found on the bottom of her supercute Skecher. She didn't say "ew" out loud, but it was implied.

I was all, *Nope, nope, nope! Screw "be friendly." Life's too short! I am done with this stuck-up wanker.* I didn't speak to her again. I didn't need to be told twice how little I counted.

"Let's get started," Emberleigh said, gazing over my head.

Pax was right about the tour. We didn't see anything out of the ordinary during the school tour. The only snafu was in the art room. Emberleigh pointed out her *ah-may-zing* sculpture she made over the summer.

"I was privileged enough to be invited to join the Advanced Ceramics: Process and Practice class this summer. Only a handful of incoming freshmen had the honor. It's part of the gifted curriculum," Emberleigh said, taking the humble straight out of humblebrag.

Mom said, "It's a beautiful squirrel, Emberleigh." Poor Mom. She was trying so hard to please Emberleigh. I squinted my eyes, because I didn't see a squirrel. I saw a hamster. Maybe a ferret.

"It's a marmot," Emberleigh said, all prissy.

"A marmot," Mom said, looking closer. "Of course. I see it now. The face is perfect."

"You're looking at the back of it."

"Right." Mom frowned. "What's a marmot?" she whispered to me.

A dad in the group chuckled softly and his wife *shh'd* him hard.

"Where's the cafeteria?" I asked.

Emberleigh ignored me (again!) and looked at her phone. "No more questions. We're out of time. Mr. Cutler wants to speak to all the parents at 7:40. We need to head back to the multipurpose room."

See? I told you she's the worst, right?

Just in case I wasn't completely done with Emberleigh, at the end of our tour Big Hair Three came up and whispered something in her ear and then they both looked at me like something on the bottom of Emberleigh's supercute Skecher and said "ew" with their piercing blue eyes. With the two of them standing side by side, I realized the resemblance couldn't be denied. Big Hair Three was the brainiac who came up with the dumbest name on the planet: Emberleigh.

So, to sum up: Mom and I have BOTH already made enemies and school hasn't even started.

Plum's Punch List:

1. Candy crushing coach
2. Big Hair Three
3. Emberleigh
4. Lack of pine trees around SPHS
5. Rawr!

Wednesday

August 17

Mom and Dad thought I was in bed, but I got up to get a snack and I overheard them talking about Big Hair Three and Emberleigh.

"You don't understand this woman," Mom said. "She is truly the meanest person I've ever met."

Dad snorted. "Come on, Lily. You tend to exaggerate when you're upset."

"I'm not exaggerating. She wouldn't even shake my hand. She's a pearl-clutcher. She's like that woman from Nebraska or South Dakota—remember her? Where was she from?"

"Who are you talking about?" Dad asked.

"You know, the one who hated me so much that she sent back her copy of *The Elf Who Did It On The Shelf*—"

"Is that one of your Christmas books?"

"It was Merry Coitus Christmas Volume Three, actually."

"Okay."

"Anyway, remember her? She was the one who sent that book back to me with the note about how she thought was she buying a nice little story about a magical doll, but instead she got 'absolute smut' and she couldn't believe that anyone actually paid good money for such 'trash.' Meanwhile, the pages were tattered and the spine was broken. Ha! For someone who said she couldn't stomach my writing, she sure did read a lot of it!"

"Yeah, I kind of remember her," Dad prodded. "Anyway, what does she have to do with the woman you met at the school?"

"Well, that Nebraska woman and that PTA psycho are exactly the same. They're hypocrites! They cry and clutch their pearls and talk about their delicate sensibilities—and the *children*, oh the children!—but meanwhile, they *wish* a Christmas elf would ravage them!"

Dad sputtered. "The Christmas elf ravages women?" he asked a bit horrified. "That's what you wrote about?"

Mom slugged him in the arm. "Duh. As if you didn't know."

"I really didn't." Dad never reads Mom's books. He says until she writes those ten-pound books about government assassins and espionage, he's not interested.

"I mean, it's all consensual. They *want* the elf!"

"Uh-huh," Dad said, but I could hear the concern in his voice. "But it's an *elf*."

"You're losing the thread here, Ben!" Mom said. "What I'm saying is these types of women, I really didn't think they existed, and left their homes in the daylight. I thought they lived in dark basements and trolled people on the Internet. I've never actually met one in person. Until yesterday. You should have seen her, looking down her perfect nose on us."

"Her 'perfect nose'?" Dad asked. "I think that's the third time you've used the word perfect to describe this woman."

"So?" Mom huffed.

"So maybe you were feeling a little insecure around this woman, Lily. Maybe you're imagining behavior that isn't there. Maybe you're a little—" Dad hesitated, "—jealous."

"Jealous!" Mom screeched. *Uh-oh*, I thought. Dad was treading on *very* thin ice. Mom does not compare herself to other women, and she prides herself on being perfectly fine with who she is and owning all her imperfections and flaws and loving them, and blah, blah, blah. Dad should have known better. "No doubt this woman has stirred up many feelings, but jealousy is not one of them. There is nothing to be jealous of! She's so—so—so—fake. I wouldn't want to be so plastic!" Mom sputtered. "She and her friends were carbon copies of one another, sharing one hive brain between the three of them. Even her personality was store-bought. I think they sell them wholesale at Costco."

Dad held up his hands in surrender. "Fine, whatever you say, Lily," he soothed.

"And her daughter! Ugh. The way she treated Plum."

"Wait. Her daughter is mean too?" Dad asked.

"Yes! That's what I've been trying to tell you! Look, I can deal with the mother. Let's face it, I probably will never see her again, but poor Plum has to go to school every day with *Emberleigh*."

"That is not her name," Dad said, chuckling.

"It is!"

"No wonder she's a snot. Imagine the teasing she must get. Maybe she's troubled, Lily. Maybe it will be a chance for Plum to reach out to a student in need."

Mom sighed heavily. "Ben, *Plum* is the student in need! Don't you get it? Haven't you been listening to me at all? Emberleigh might have been cool to Plum, but then her mother got a hold of her. I saw them whispering and staring. It's all my fault. Why can't I be a normal mom who volunteers at the school and has a part-time job as a receptionist in a doctor's office?" Mom wailed.

"Is Emberleigh's mom a part-time receptionist?"

"I don't know, Ben! Why would you ask me that? Who cares what she does?"

"Lily." Dad sounded exasperated. "I'm just trying to understand the drama here."

"The *drama* is Plum's new school experience is going to be a disaster because of me!"

"Oh come on." Dad sighed. "You do this a lot, Lily. Plum's inability to fit in is not caused by you."

Well...I wouldn't say Mom *helps* in that department.

"You have no idea what sort of impact I have on the kids!" Mom wailed.

Oh great. Here we go again, I thought. Dad's right. Mom does do this a lot.

Every once in a while Mom goes off on a tangent that her job is going to cause problems for me and Pax—or "impact" us. She takes her job very seriously and she gets super crazy.

I know, I know. The way she acts you'd think she had some kind of top-secret dangerous job like a CIA agent. Or a completely heinous job like someone who euthanizes stray dogs. Get a grip, Mom.

There have always been people who don't like what Mom does for a living, but we've really never had to interact with them on a daily basis. It has never *impacted* me. Mom has never lied to us about what she does. She's proud of it. She loves her job. She always wanted to be a writer, and she tried writing all different kinds of books (except dystopian, no matter how much I beg). Her kissing books are the ones that took off and so that's what she writes now. She uses the pen name Lacy Drawers so she can sort of stay private, but she does a lot of events for her readers and her picture is out there, so it's only kind of private. She's got like 12 million people who follow her on Facebook. I'm not even exaggerating. Who knew there were that many people still on Facebook?? Honestly, I didn't even realize Facebook was still a thing. Her followers call themselves Lacy's Lovelies. I know, barf, right? They named themselves and Mom didn't even try to rename them. She thinks it's cute.

Every now and again people recognize her. When they do, they're usually superfans of hers. They get really crazy excited, actually. They want to take pictures with her or have her sign something. One time we were at Target and one of her Lovelies accosted Mom in the toilet paper aisle.

"Lacy! Lacy!" the woman cried. "You saved my marriage! My husband wasn't interested in … (she glanced at me) … maintaining our *relations*. He was behaving just like Jaysun and then I realized he had PTSD and low testosterone just like Jaysun did! He saw a doctor and we're doing so much better now. I can't thank you enough."

I was eating delicious Target popcorn at the time and I almost choked to death after hearing her confession. Just like that, a stranger started talking about her bedroom antics in the middle of the toilet paper aisle in Target! Who does that?? Mom didn't even have the decency to look embarrassed. The woman asked Mom to take a selfie with her. Mom looked like crap. She wasn't wearing makeup, she hadn't showered in probably two days ("One of the perks of the job!" she says), and she was wearing one of Dad's holey T-shirts, but she smiled the hugest smile ever and said, "You bet!" and then she signed the lady's roll of toilet paper. What in the Hello Kitty? Living the dream, Mom!

I know not everyone is a fan of what Mom writes. I've heard her and Dad talk about hate mail she gets sometimes or bad reviews online, and I know about the woman and the Elf book. She was actually from South Dakota, but details aren't important to Mom. But before today Mom has never let those things bother her. I could tell Big Hair Three had really bothered her. This was going to be a problem. Mom was right, I was the one who had to deal with Emberleigh and her friends, but I knew Mom would somehow figure out how to make this mess all about her. She always did. I mean, look at her! I can't even be socially awkward because I'm a weirdo. Instead I must be socially awkward because my mom writes porn!

I went back to my room (without a snack, because her drama ruined my appetite) and fell down the rabbit hole that is Emberleigh Davidson's social media. I needed to know my enemy. All I can say is I would like those two—four—hours back ASAP.

Soooo many duck-lipped selfies or faux-inspirational quotes about being bold and dreaming big and shit like that. She's a fanatic about seashells and can't stop posting pictures of seashells. What's that all about? She does realize she lives in a landlocked state, right? Does she go to the ocean, like, once a year or something and take 365 photos of seashells so she can post a new one each day? Her Insta's flooded with tags from her minions (#squad) and her mom. God, her mom! It's like no one else has ever had a daughter before Mrs. Davidson. And I don't think she knows any hashtag other than #blessed. Don't get me wrong, I know Mom loves me, I just don't need her to share that love with the entire world. #barf

I don't even understand people like her. Emberleigh's social media was so filtered (even though her second-favorite hashtag is #nofilter) that you can only see a snippet of what she is really like. If you were only judging her by her social media you'd think she's a pretty decent human being. She appears to be someone who is motivated, has high self-esteem, and loves nature. She's got great friends and a mom who adores her. But I could see through all that phoniness. Emberleigh has been very deliberate about which parts of her life she lets the world see. They only get to see the filtered, Photoshopped, perfect side of her. It's only when you interact with her on a personal level do you get a glimpse of the real her: the stuck-up, judgmental, conceited side.

Emberleigh is going to be a huge pain in the ass. I can tell. But I won't let Mom know. I won't tell her. I don't want to upset her. She's not thrilled with Kansas either, and I could see last night when she was interacting with the Big Hairs that she's just as awkward as me. She tries to hide it, but she has trouble fitting in too. The other moms don't get her. I can't burden her with my troubles. I just won't let Emberleigh bother me. With my luck, I'll be invisible to her.

Plum's Punch List:

1. Emberleigh (I have a feeling she's going to make the list a lot this year)
2. Facebook (how is it still a thing??)

Thursday

August 18

Crap. I'm not invisible to Emberleigh.

Not even close.

Let me explain: today was the first day of school and it blew chunks. The number 2,457,875 thing that sucks about Kansas: school starts in August.

Awful, right? I can't even right now. In New Jersey I went to school until June and suddenly I was back again. It's so unfair. It's beyond unfair. It's like a punishment for something I didn't even do. Sooo uncool.

Anyhoo, I woke up this morning with the plan that I'd just try to blend in and to disappear, but it just didn't work.

I was going to wear the shirt Kennedy and I had picked out for the first day of school, but after taking a second look at it, I decided to branch out a bit. I was trying to make a fresh start. A new impression. I wanted to try something new. That dumb popular list had said:

38. Get your own fashionable style. Embrace the trends, but make them your OWN!

A black T-shirt and blue jeans were not really fashionable. I needed to step up my game a bit. A few days ago I made Mom take me shopping. Well, "made" is a strong word. Mom doesn't need anyone to twist her arm to make her hit the mall. You know how some moms work out every day at a gym and all the employees know her name? That's how Mom is at the mall. We've only been here a couple of weeks and she's already made herself a regular at every single mall in a twenty-mile radius.

Mom and I hit just about every single "teenager" store out there. She bought me new jeans, a bunch of tops, and some really awesome boots. Not cowboy boots, but like boot boots—ass-kicking boots. I was looking at some T-shirts in one store. They had a bunch of old-timey bands on them: Nirvana, The Cure, Duran Duran, Siouxsie and the Banshees. I'd never heard of any of the bands, but the shirts seemed cool and so I wanted them. Mom FLIPPED out. She was like, "I OWN THESE!" She was so excited to finally have something I wanted.

When we got home she dug a box out of the basement that was full of T-shirts like the ones I'd seen at the mall and then some. They were pretty cool, actually, because they were like *real* antiques. The distressed hems on them were actually distressed from time and stuff.

So, for the first day of school, I picked out one of Mom's shirts (Bananarama, mostly because it's fun to say), a new pair of jeans, my sweet boot boots, and a hat I'd found in one of Mom's boxes. I think she called it a beret.

I was surveying my ensemble in the full-length mirror when Pax poked his head in my room. "Hey, are you re—whoa!" he said.

"What?"

"That is what you're wearing today?" he asked.

"Yes," I sniffed. I looked him up and down. He was wearing his usual uniform of swishy shorts (i.e., yoga pants for boys) and a T-shirt advertising a fundraising event at our elementary school in New Jersey. *This is the guy questioning my outfit?* I thought. I might not have found a signature scent, but I'd definitely found my fashionable style.

"I mean, I guess the jeans are okay and the boots are…something else. What happened to your Converse?"

"I'm trying something new," I said.

"Is that Mom's shirt?" he asked, wrinkling his nose.

"It's *antique*, moron," I sneered.

"I think you mean vintage," he said.

"Fine. Whatever." I went back to fixing my beret.

"Yeah, can we at least talk about the hat, Plum?"

I was pissed at him. Okay, I'll be honest, I wasn't really feeling the beret myself; it was a little odd-looking and sort of mushed my hair and looked like it would never stay on my head all day. But I was putting myself out there! I was trying something new! Sometimes it can be uncomfortable to be a trendsetter! Someone has to have the confidence to be first and that was me, thank you very much! And I didn't appreciate his tone. The beret shifted a bit on my head and threatened to fall off. I grabbed it before he could notice. *Screw him,* I thought. Whatever he was going to say was probably right, but I wasn't going to encourage him, so I said, "I love it."

Pax looked surprised. "You do?"

"Yeah. Why wouldn't I?"

"I dunno. It's just not your usual look. Plus, it takes a ... special person to pull off a hat like that."

"I'm reinventing myself," I reminded him. "The new Plum wears interesting and unusual hats! She's trendy!"

"So that's trendy?" Pax asked.

Oh for goodness' sake! I ask you, what does Pax know about trends? Did I mention he was wearing a shirt from ELEMENTARY SCHOOL? How did that shirt still even fit him?

Mom interrupted us. "You ready to go?"

"I'm ready," Pax said. "I'm not sure about Plum ..."

"Oh, Pax," Mom said, all weepyish. "You're wearing your shirt from the George Washington Elementary School Fun Run."

"Huh?" Pax grunted. He looked at his shirt as if it was the first time he'd even realized what he was wearing. "Oh, yeah."

"I can't believe it still fits you," Mom said, petting it. "You were so little when we bought it."

Pax shrugged. "Well, when you order an adult extra large instead of a children's extra large, it fits you for a long time."

I started giggling. "I'd forgotten that she did that to both of us."

"Dad wanted to get his money's worth," Mom said, shrugging.

"I thought you didn't read closely and marked the wrong box," I said.

Mom shrugged. "Yeah, that also sounds plausible. Either way, it's washed beautifully over the years."

Pax smiled. "Remember, Plum, you belted yours and wore it like a dress."

"See? Even then I was a fashion maker," I teased.

Pax threw an arm around my shoulder and pulled me close. "You've always been an individual, Plum. That's for sure."

Pax hadn't been so affectionate to me in months. It surprised the heck out of me. I could tell Mom was shocked too and she wanted to pull out her phone and take a picture, but thank goodness she refrained. Instead she focused on my hat. "It doesn't sit on the top of your head like that, Plum. You have to kind of angle it," Mom said, adjusting the beret. "How's that?"

I looked in the mirror. I still wasn't feeling the hat completely, but it did look better. I needed that hat. My roots are growing out and there's something about the humidity here in Kansas that's wreaking havoc on my hair. Even the flat iron isn't cutting it most days, so my hair is always kind of a frizzy mess. The hat covered a lot of problems. "Perfect," I replied dubiously.

"I think it looks great," Mom said. "You do you, Plum."

Mom drove us to school and reluctantly dropped me and Pax at the front door of SPHS. She wanted to walk us in and help us find our lockers. I begged her to kill me instead.

"Seriously, Mom, just put an ice pick in my brain. It would be a far less painful death than having my mommy walk me to my locker."

"I don't like to encourage Plum's theatrics," Pax said. "but I'm inclined to agree with her on this one, Mom."

"Fine! But remember, kids," Mom said. "Be positive, feel positive! And don't forget to be—"

"Awesome!" Pax and I said in unison, rolling our eyes.

We got out of the car and I was shocked to see a red carpet running from the carpool drop-off spot to the front doors of the school.

Literally.

A.

Red.

Carpet.

Someone had gone out and bought a red carpet for students to walk on the first day of school. That's when I realized the teachers and staff were lined up along both sides of the red carpet cheering wildly for us. And roaring. (Of course they were.) Go, Pumas!

A woman stepped out of the cluster of teachers and started snapping pictures of me and Pax.

"Work it!" she yelled.

Work it??? AYFKM?

I looked back to see if Mom had driven away yet. I wanted to dive back into the minivan and demand she homeschool me, but she was long gone. She puts up a good front about how sad she is when we go back to school, but I knew she was rushing home to revel in the quiet solitude of our house.

I willed myself to spontaneously combust, but no dice. So, I ducked behind Pax and tried to hustle him into the school as quickly as possible.

We walked into the lobby and I was immediately overwhelmed by the noise and activity. Gaggles of girls fixing each other's hair and squealing at decibel levels that could drive howler monkeys insane hung out on one side of the room making side-eyes at boys who ignored them completely. The boys were far more interested in exchanging elaborate handshakes that included snaps, chest bumps, and high fives.

Pax was immediately engulfed by a crew of bros, (How does that he do that?????) leaving me completely alone in the desolate no man's land of the middle of the room.

The bell hadn't rung yet, so everyone was hanging out around the rows of lockers. Loose packs of like-minded individuals formed and I tried to see where I might fit:

Nerds. Lots of online role-playing talk was coming from that group. I could maybe be a Nerd if I created a hot female avatar for myself and joined their game. But that would mean I'd need to know the difference between trolls and elves and that sounded like homework.

Geeks. Not to be confused with Nerds. The Geeks are all about grades.

They take accelerated math and science courses and build robots in their spare time. They plan to rule the world someday and make the rest of us work for them. I'm not smart enough to be a Geek.

Burn-outs. This group sees absolutely no value in education—or anything that doesn't get them high. I'm too afraid to be a burn-out. I have an addictive personality, and I think one hit of whatever they're huffing would turn me into a full-blown addict living under an overpass.

Girly-Girls. Those are the kinds of girls who know what a signature scent is and actually have one. No matter how hard I tried, I could never be girly enough to please them.

Bromancers. That's Pax's domain. They have elaborate handshakes and they say stuff like, "I love you, man." When you join, your name is instantly forgotten and you're forever known simply as "Bro."

Jocks. Hahahahahahahaha. I can't kick, catch, or throw a ball and I could run MAYBE if a serial killer was chasing me. Hard pass.

Artsy Fartsies. I'm usually drawn to these people. I should be one of them. I like to draw and I can be just as emo as the next girl. But when you take a closer look you can see it requires a crap ton of commitment to be so darn depressing all the time. Believe it or not, I am too upbeat for that bunch.

Wallflowers. Let's face it, try as I might to fit into any other group, *those* three or four kids scattered around the room propping up walls and speaking to no one were my people.

I was just about to take my place near the corner (it was vacant and looked like it could use my services) when I heard a teacher say, "No hats, young lady."

I looked around wildly. Was she talking to me? "Excuse me?"

The teacher came closer. "No hats in the building. It's a rule."

"No hats?" I sputtered.

"No. Hats," she said, and then she reached out and snatched the beret off my head.

"WAIT!" I screamed. But I was too late, I could feel my hair literally exploding in a frizzy halo around my head. It's like my hair let out a big sigh of relief and poofed out. "NOOOOO!"

I heard someone call out, "Look, it's Pinky Dinky Doo!"

Motherclucker! Not only did I have atrocious hat-head, my once-glorious bubblegum-pink hair was fading into a dusty mauve. I needed a touch-up ASAP, but Mom hadn't found a stylist yet. I couldn't believe I hadn't insisted on her making it a priority before the first day of school. Mauve was *not* the look I was going for. The pink was so much cooler. No one would make fun of my hair if the color was fresh! I smoothed my hair down as best I could. I would just have to embrace the poofiness and make it part of my new, unique style. Besides, I was sure no one would notice. It wasn't that bad. I was wrong.

"What's up, Strawberry Shortcake?" somebody yelled.

It was like all these jackalopes brought their annoying-ness to school today and they were directing it all at me.

The bell rang and everyone started migrating toward the wheel spokes (I later found out they're called "pods," because that's not creepy-sounding at all).

I fell in line with the zombie shuffle when Mr. Cutler stepped in my path. "Good morning, Plum," he said. "Are you ready for a great day?"

I frowned at him. I felt like it was a trick question. Was it a trick question? What was the right answer? What was the wrong answer? Why did he ask *me*? Why did he single *me* out? Finally I shrugged and said, "Maybe?"

He smiled all big and I could see bits of spinach in his teeth. "Wonderful! We have a special program here at SPHS that I think would be very beneficial to you, Plum. Do you know what a peer model is?"

I couldn't focus on his words; I'd decided it was definitely broccoli in his teeth.

"When someone is new—like you, Plum—we assign a peer model to them. This person has the same schedule as you and she'll eat lunch with you today. She'll help you get better acquainted with our school and make your day go a little easier."

"Umm … great," I said. I couldn't take my eyes off the kale (??) in his teeth.

"You've been assigned to one of our most impressive students. She's the head of our peer modeling program, she's a school ambassador, she's the ninth-grade class president, the lead soprano in the choir, and captain of the junior varsity cheerleaders...word vomit, word vomit, she saves baby seals, she's researching a cure for cancer, and she's up for a Nobel Prize." Okay, he didn't actually say all those things, but it was pretty bad. You get the gist. He did end with, "Simply put, she is a treasure to our school." True story, he said "treasure to our school."

Maybe I didn't understand what the word "peer" meant. I thought it meant someone who is like you. I needed Mr. Cutler to hook me up with an awkward, underachieving girl with coral-colored hair and a permanent scowl. Someone who could give me the info on how to get an excused absence from gym, like does "I'm on my lady days" count or do I need to fake a real injury? The peer model I'd been assigned to sounded awful. Almost as bad as...

Emberleigh.

Yup. You guessed it. My peer model is Emberleigh. ARGH!!!!

She walked up with the most sour expression on her face. Remember when she looked at me like I was something on the bottom of her supercute Skecher the other day? Well, now it looked like Mr. Cutler told her she had to *eat* what she found on the bottom of her supercute Skecher. *Le sigh.*

But that look didn't last long. As soon as Mr. Cutler turned around to greet her, that shrew got the biggest, phoniest, most fake-ass smile on her face. "Oh, Mr. Cutler! So great to see you—blah, blah, blah," she said. "How was your summer? Have you been working out?" Just utter and total butt-kissing nonsense. Pax was right, she is a principal's pet bootlicker.

The last bell rang and Mr. Cutler said, "I'll leave you in Emberleigh's incredibly capable hands, Plum. Have a great day, you two." And then he roared. Ohemgee. Is this roaring going to be a real thing people do all the time? I cannot handle having everyone growling at me. What if we were the penguins? Would everyone waddle around like a delightful flightless bird? Why must they roar?

When he walked away Emberleigh stuck out her tongue at Mr. Cutler's back. "I can't even believe this is my life right now," she said, all exasperated. Emberleigh speaks with what experts call "vocal fry." It's that low, scraggly voice that girls on TV have. I think it's the voice of privilege. It's like, "I'm so bored by my very existence that I can't even breathe right."

I wanted to say, "Take a deep breath and speak like a human," but instead I said, "Yeah."

Emberleigh continued. "My mother *specifically* requested that you be kept as far away from me as possible, and this is what he does? She's going to have his job."

"Believe me, I'm just as unhappy as you are," I said. Yeah! I said that out loud. Can you believe it? My stomach was all flip-floppy, but I didn't care. It was the truth. I wasn't lying. Why am I always so mouthy on the inside and so quiet on the outside? It felt good to stand up to her, to speak my mind. Note to self: Do that more often!

Emberleigh shot daggers with her eyes at me and my resolve faltered. *This is why I don't speak up,* I reminded myself.

I looked around for Pax. Where was he? Why didn't he get a peer model? Why was I the only sad sack with a babysitter?

"Well, let's go already!" Emberleigh said. "We can't be late for homeroom. The last thing I want is a detention with you."

"Ditto," I said. Okay, I said that pretty softly but I think she could feel my irritation. I was putting out some serious anger waves, y'know?

Plum's Punch List:

1. Hat-hair
2. Peer models
3. Mr. Cutler and his spinach/broccoli/kale-infested teeth
4. Rawr!

Friday

August 19

Please sit down, I have a very important announcement to make:

Ahem. Tap, tap, tap. Is this thing on?

I MADE A FRIEND TODAY!!!!!!!!!!!!!!!!!!!

Well, at least I think I did. Today's Friday, we'll see if we're still friends on Monday. I don't want to talk about it yet, lest I jinx myself, because let's face it, I need a friend at this point.

Badly.

Desperately.

Please check back for more details as they become available.

In the meantime, I shall let Mom take me out for celebratory mani-pedis.

Plum's Punch List:

1. Nice try, Universe. Not today!

Monday

August 22

Yup. It's official. I made a friend.

WOOOHOOO!!

His name is Oliver Bridgewater, but he likes to be called Ollie and we met when I was having lunch in the girls' bathroom.

I should probably back up and start from the beginning.

So, it was lunchtime and my awesome (is my sarcasm font working??) peer model, Emberleigh, is supposed to eat lunch with me every day, but of course she never has. I wasn't surprised the first day when she dissed me completely after Mr. Cutler handed me over to her. We were in biology when the bell rang. I was packing up my stuff, trying to think of at least five questions I could ask her. Dad says everyone should work on their conversation skills and you should always have five questions you can ask anyone. So far I had:

1. "Emberleigh, your hair is amazeballs. What kind of conditioner do you use? The tears of your enemies?"
2. "Emberleigh, do you kick puppies daily or just once a week?"
3. "Emberleigh, how do you manage to always look pissed off, bored, disgusted, and elitist all at the same time? It's truly a gift you have."

Probably not exactly what Dad had in mind. Oh well.

I was deep in thought, thinking up more questions when I looked up and Emberleigh was gone. Of course! Why would I expect anything different from that pickle on a stick?

At first I thought, *NBD, I'll eat lunch with Pax.* That's the nice thing about having a sibling at school with you. You always have a lunch buddy if you need one.

I found my way to the cafeteria (no thanks to Emberleigh), mostly by following the smell of what I can only assume was fried possum meat and rancid milk. I was expecting something similar to my old school: a big noisy room with long tables set up in rows. You could always just squeeze in somewhere. But the lunchroom at SPHS is set up completely different. It's a fairly quiet space with soft music piped in—like the kind you hear at the grocery store that's vaguely familiar but there aren't any words to remind you what terrible '80s song you're listening to. There are tables that seat two and four people. It's like the food court at the mall. Everyone pairs off with their super tight BFF group and there's no room anywhere to slide in all casual-like. I looked around the room for an empty table, but there weren't any. All I could see was Emberleigh and her band of flying monkeys sucking down baby food. Seriously. They eat baby food. I overheard Glynis talking about it in social studies. They think it's healthy and low calorie or something. "Plus, it's, like, so much better for you not to chew so much. Chewing is really, like, hard on your jaw and can cause wrinkles later in life," Kalista told a wide-eyed devotee who nodded along like everything Kalista said made perfect sense. So bizarre. The baby food bingers caught me looking at them and they started snickering. Emberleigh smiled all evil, but the joke was on her because she was eating pureed peas or something and her teeth were green.

I spotted Pax. He was at a table with three other boys, deep in conversation about lacrosse or NBA draft picks probably. I picked my way across the cafeteria and came up behind Pax.

"Hey," I said.

He looked up. "Hey, Plum," he said. "How's it going?"

"Okay. I'm a little hungry," I said, hoping he'd get the hint I wanted to join him.

"Yeah," he said. "You'd better find a seat quick. Lunch is only twenty minutes long. You don't want to spend the whole time looking for a place to sit, right? I'll see you later, Plummy." He turned back to his wannabe frat boys and left me standing there staring at the back of his head. What. The. Hell. Man? Sometimes he's so thick! I'm convinced he got all the looks, but I got all the brains.

Emberleigh and her green teeth were mocking me, so I decided I'd had enough mortification for the day and I escaped to my favorite lunchtime haunt: the girls' bathroom.

I'm not proud of this fact, but over the years I've eaten my lunch in the girls' bathroom more times than I care to admit. Just hear me out:

There's always a seat.

The handicapped stall is actually quite roomy.

It's quiet.

And I see the janitors cleaning the bathroom more often than the lunchroom, so I'm convinced it's the cleaner of the two.

So, I set up shop in the handicapped stall and spent the fifteen minutes I had left scarfing down my PB&J while sending an email to Kennedy updating her on the Emberleigh/Kansas saga that is now my life.

Side note: I've sent Kennedy close to fifty emails and text messages since I moved to Kansas. She's replied to precisely two. I'm not sure what gives, but I don't have the bandwidth to deal with that drama right now too. I'm barely holding it together as it is.

Anyhoo, the bell rang and I wasn't quite done writing my email, so I was typing furiously and walking at the same time. I shoved open the door to the bathroom and charged out, running right into someone charging out of the boys' room across the hallway.

We both fell on our butts, papers and books flying everywhere. My phone skittered across the floor and hit the wall. Kennedy made me watch rom-coms with her and she gets all swoony when the boy and girl meet for the first time. It's always something silly like bumping into one another or he spills something on her or she insults him. If Kennedy were there she would have said my collision was absolutely rom-com-dorable. I grabbed my phone and

JEN MANN

checked for damage and then I got my papers and whatnot picked up. After a minute, I finally looked at who I'd run into. Kennedy's romantic notions have rubbed off on me so much that I half expected to see my dashing future husband standing there grinning mischievously at me. Instead, I saw a slender boy with a nose ring wearing a T-shirt that said, "I Speak Sarcasm Fluently."

"OH. EMM. GEE," the boy exclaimed. "Your hair is absolutely *ah-may-ze* balls."

"Oh!" I said, smiling and fluffing it a bit.

"The color is fading a bit, but I can tell is was once gorg," he said. "But that cut is kind of awful for your face shape."

"Wait," I said mid-fluff. "What did you just say to me?"

"It's okay, don't worry. I can totally help you," he promised.

Even though I should have been offended by his completely unwarranted comments on my hair, I wasn't. I totally forgave Oliver because he was right. The color was once "gorg" and the cut had grown out into a hot mess and the humidity was wreaking havoc and I was letting it win. Also, that's when I realized it didn't matter how rom-com-dorable we met, Oliver was never going to be my husband, because Oliver was clearly gay. I knew it as soon as he opened his mouth and commented on my coif. In all of my fourteen years on this planet, I've never met a boy with an opinion about my hair. I knew his status before he said, "Hi! I'm Oliver Bridgewater, but everyone calls me Ollie. I'm gay and if that's a problem for you, then see ya."

I didn't know what to say. I'm pretty sure I stood there for a full thirty seconds with my mouth hanging open. Being gay isn't a problem for me—I don't think. I mean, to be honest, I've never had a gay friend before and I wasn't sure how to react. BTW, Ollie says statistically that's not true. I have had gay friends before, but they just never felt comfortable telling me. He says he used to be like that too. But he recently ran out of fucks to give. He just says what he thinks now and he's up front with everyone so he knows where he stands with them. "Life is too short to surround myself with humpback troglodytes!" he said. I had no idea what that meant, but it sounded sooooo cool. Ollie says he prefers to use "educated" insults rather than lowering himself to words like "stupid." He has a Shakespearean insult generator app

108

on his phone. I need to ask Mom and Dad if I can download one too.

All I knew was even the Wallflowers had made it clear there weren't enough walls for all of us to hold up. I needed a friend and so did Ollie. I could see neither of us fit into the already established groups. We'd need to start our own. Finally I spoke. I said, "I'm Plum Parrish. I think I might be invisible. You're truly the first person who has spoken to me all day who wasn't related to me, a teacher, or an administrator."

"I can assure you that you're not invisible, Plum Parrish. I see you," Ollie said, linking his arm through mine.

He walked me to my locker and told me his whole life story: He's new too (yay!). He came at the end of the school year in eighth grade and he still hasn't made any friends (boo!). He thinks Kansas is kind of strange too. He's from Alabama, and the people here make fun of his accent. He doesn't live with his parents. When he told them he was gay, his "daddy" (his word, not mine) couldn't handle it, so he sent him to live with his "MeeMaw" (also his word) in Kansas. He says his daddy still loves him and is praying for him, though, hoping he'll see the light and love girls instead of boys. Once he loves girls he's welcome to come home again, but until that happens, his daddy isn't interested in having Ollie live with him—EVER.

"So," Ollie said, shrugging. "Looks like I'll be here for a while."

WHOA.

That was a lot to unload on the first meeting, but I guess I'm glad Ollie trusted me enough to tell me. The problem was I had no idea what to say. I'm not sure how Dad and Mom would react if Pax or I told them we were gay. I'd like to think they'd accept us, but suddenly I wasn't so sure. I mean, I just always thought parents accept everything you do. Yes, you do things that are not what they expected or you upset them, but they're supposed to love you no matter what. They're supposed to accept you and help you get through your rough patches. I can't imagine my parents just turning me out and sending me to live with my grandma. I don't even like my grandma that much, so I'd be double miserable!

"Listen to me!" Ollie said, clapping a hand over his mouth. "I'll just babble on and on until you tell me to shut up, Plum. I'm done taking up all of the oxygen in the room. Your turn. Tell me why you were eating lunch in the bathroom."

"You knew I was eating in there?" I asked.

"You have peanut butter on your cheek."

"Of course I do." I sighed, rubbing my cheek. "At least I didn't drop a blob of jelly down the front of my shirt, because that's what I normally do." I considered what I should tell Ollie. After all, my drama felt infinitesimal compared to his, but he was standing there, seeing me. Hearing me. Listening. So, I vented my spleen. It had been a long day and Kennedy's radio silence was making me bottle up a lot of stuff and I needed to let some of it out before I exploded. I told him about Kennedy and Madame O'Malley and French Club and Emberleigh and her mom and my mom and my brother and how I ended up eating PB&J in the girls' bathroom.

"Boy, I thought I had a lot going on," Ollie said sympathetically. It did not make me feel better to know that Ollie thought my problems were bigger than his.

When we got to my social studies class Ollie said, "Hey! Let's eat lunch together on Monday. Like normal people—in the cafeteria." I must have looked a little worried about Emberleigh and company, because he said, "Be brave, Plum! You can't let those milk-livered, onion-eyed scoundrels get to you." And with a flourish, he turned on his heel and headed to geometry.

And so today we had lunch together. Ollie is officially my Kansas BFF. I wish Kennedy would answer my emails so I could tell her about him.

Plum's Punch List:

1. SPHS lunch room
2. SPHS girls' bathroom
3. PB&J (I need to tell Mom to buy some lunch meat or something)
4. Emberleigh (shocker)

Thursday

August 25

I saw Emberleigh and her pack of piranhas patrolling the halls. (Can you tell we've been working on alliteration in English class? Sometimes I can't help myself!) They were all dressed alike. Being dressed alike is really nothing new for those dolts. They like to wear different shades of the same color on the same day. Like Emberleigh wears dark pink and then Savannah (her number 2) wears a shade just a tad lighter and then Kalista goes one shade lighter and then finally Glynis. Glynis is so low on the totem pole, she's basically wearing a dingy sweater that looks like it was once white and then it accidentally got washed with a load of pinks. Emberleigh calls their coordinated look "ombre." I call it "paint chip," because they look like one of those strips you get from the hardware store.

Anyhoo, they weren't dressed in ombre ensembles, instead they were all in cheerleading costumes—oops, I should probably call them uniforms seeing as they're legit athletes or whatever. Their uniforms consisted of short skirts, tight, midriff-baring tops, and the biggest bows I've ever seen in their flawless bouffants. Seriously, their bows were bigger than their heads—and their shirts. I don't know if that's a Kansas thing or a cheerleading thing. On closer inspection, I could see that Emberleigh's bow was just a smidge bigger than everyone else's. OF COURSE it was. That girl must lord her superiority over her stooges in any way that she can.

So, they were in their *uniforms* and they were acting more arrogant than usual if that were possible. A girl in a headscarf accidentally bumped into Emberleigh and she bit the girl's head off. Like, almost literally. She snapped her jaws at the poor girl like something out of a zombie movie.

"Watch where you're going, you moron!" she sneered.

"Sorry," the girl mumbled. "It was an accident."

"It better be!" Emberleigh said. She turned to Kalista. "God! Why doesn't anyone look where they're going?"

"Maybe her scarf slipped down over her eyes," Glynis said. They all laughed.

At that point, I'd had enough. I could feel my pulse race, and my hands started to shake. *Why are they such bitches? Why doesn't anyone tell them go to hell?* I thought. That's when I went up to Emberleigh and her flunkies and asked, "Is it Halloween or something? Why are you guys wearing those dumb costumes?"

Emberleigh turned so red I thought maybe her head just might explode. Now, *that* would have been something to see, right!? Instead, she turned to Savannah and said, "I'm exhausted. I can't even with these people right now. Handle this, Savannah." And that's when Savannah let me know they weren't wearing costumes. They were wearing uniforms, thank you very much! She also told me that the four of them are the coolest girls on the junior varsity cheerleading squad and if I knew anything about anything, I'd know that. She informed me they were wearing their uniforms because they were performing at the first pep rally of the season. She also let me know I was really annoying her. Her exact words were, "You're a waste of space, Plum Parrish. You should probably kill yourself."

I was about to invite her to eat a bag of dicks when Principal Cutler came over the PA system. "Good afternoon, Pumas!" he yelled.

I could hear the students and staff—seriously, staff??—around me roar.

"RAWRRR!"

A teacher glared at me, so I made a halfhearted swipe with my paw and moved my mouth.

Mr. Cutler kept going. "It's time for everyone to proceed in an orderly fashion to the gym for our first pep rally of the year!"

Everyone around me flung open their lockers and started packing up their bags, chatting excitedly. Emberleigh and her flock of fangirls disappeared.

I don't really get pep rallies. I have never thought it sounded like a fun time to sit on uncomfortable bleachers and watch a bunch of pimply assclowns break through a paper wall while fanatic acolytes lose their ever-loving minds and show their devotion by screaming so loudly your eardrums threaten to rupture. At my old school you could skip pep rallies. You could go to the library and work on your homework or you could go home. I assumed SPHS was the same and since I didn't have any homework, I decided to go home.

The masses headed one way and I ducked out the back door and headed for home. I didn't take three steps outside the building before a deep voice yelled, "Hey, you! Young lady with the…er…pink hair. Stop!"

I turned around and saw a burly man with a mustache coming after me. At first I was little concerned. Usually if a big dude is chasing you, the last thing you want to do is stop and let him catch you. But I could see an official school ID badge swinging around his neck, so I figured he was bona fide and I slowed down.

"Where do you think you're going?" he asked me, all huffing and puffing.

I shrugged. "Home," I said.

"The day's not over yet."

I shrugged again. "It's just a dumb pep rally. What is the point anyway? Why are we expected to cheer for a gang of goofballs just because they can run a little faster or a catch a few more balls than the average bear? Why does our society glorify sports instead of the arts and sciences? When will there be pep rallies for the debate team or the science club? I'll stay and cheer on that day."

It took all the restraint I had not to slap a hand over my mouth. I couldn't believe I was so brazen! I had no idea what had gotten into me. Apparently my altercation with Savannah had broken some kind of dam inside me, and it wasn't going to get repaired any time soon, I've never mouthed off to a teacher before in my life. I was sure it wasn't going to go well for me, but I didn't care. I just waited for the hammer.

The huffing-puffing guy didn't say anything, but his mustache twitched. I couldn't tell if he was fighting off a grin or a frown. "I don't care what you think of pep rallies," he said finally. "But this is a closed campus. No one leaves until the final bell rings. Now, head to the gym."

He must have thought I looked kind of shady, because instead of trusting me to go to the gym on my own, he escorted me the entire way. Probably a smart move since we passed, like, four more doors where I could have bailed.

We got to the doors of the gym and I sighed heavily. He patted my shoulder sympathetically. "It's only thirty minutes, kiddo," he said, opening the door and nudging me through. "Trust me, you'll survive."

I stomped across the threshold. As I had feared, the noise was deafening and the entire room shook from the hundreds of stomping feet. I looked around briefly for Ollie but didn't see him. I didn't look that hard, because frankly I don't like to stand in front of a group of strangers and be the center of attention. You know how people have that nightmare of being naked in front of the class or whatever? My nightmare is standing in front of a room full of strangers and have them watch me look for a friendly face and then judge me when I don't see one. I'm sure no one even noticed me, but my brain was telling me everyone was watching me scan the rows for Ollie and they were all laughing at me because I have no friends. (I tend to flatter myself a lot thinking anyone actually sees me.)

I saw some empty rows near the top. I abandoned my search for Ollie and headed there. I settled in and pulled a book out of my backpack along with my phone and earbuds. My body had to be present, but nobody had said anything about my mind.

I was about two pages in when I realized someone was talking to me. "Hey, look who it is! It's Pinky Dinky Doo again!"

I looked around and saw a boy who can only be described as a "future frat boy who flunks out of college and is forced to work for his dad for the rest of his life." I rolled my eyes. I couldn't be bothered to respond to him. I went back to my book.

"Hey, Pinkalicious! I'm talking to you!"

I looked up again. His face was contorted in fury. I'm guessing this entitled brat has never been ignored in his life. This was a boy who had been told since birth he's exceptional and his opinion matters just a hair more than anyone else's. He probably has a whole shelf full of participation trophies his mommy dusts for him every week.

"Maybe I should call you Pinkie Pie!" he said. "'Cause you look like a horse!" His henchmen guffawed and nodded.

What did I do to him to deserve this treatment? I wondered. Let me break this down. I had been invisible since I set foot in SPHS and now suddenly this boy had taken an unnatural interest in me. Why?? Honestly, I didn't have the brainpower to deal with him. Plus, I'd already made enough enemies for the day, so I decided to hear what he had to say. I pulled out my earbuds. "All right," I said, putting a bookmark in my book. "I'm listening."

"Where's your school pride?" he sneered. "First you come in late and then you sit here and read a book with your earbuds in?"

His pack of wilding friends turned their beady eyes on me. Suddenly, I felt like a cornered animal. If I had hackles, they would have risen.

"I'm new," I said, hoping that answer would suffice.

"So what?" Frat Boy said, taking a step closer to me. "That's not an excuse."

Merde, I thought. *I should not have engaged.*

The crowd around us erupted in a fervor. The bleachers shook and I couldn't hear any more of Frat Boy's insults over the din. Emberleigh and the rest of the cheerleaders tumbled across the floor. Savannah did five back handsprings in a row and Glynis did this really complicated-looking routine that ended with her in the splits on the shoulders of two other cheerleaders.

I must admit, I was hella impressed. Those girls are athletes! However, I've never understood cheerleading. When I was seven, Mom and Dad enrolled me in a cheerleading camp for a week. It was run by the high school team. They were supposed to teach us a few simple cheers. I really liked the jumping and yelling parts. But at the end of the week we had to go to a football game to actually cheer with the team. It was a freezing night and we were out there in our short skirts hopping around mostly so we wouldn't turn into actual blocks of ice. I could see Mom and Dad in the stands waving at me and taking pictures, but then I realized they were the ONLY PEOPLE watching us! Everyone else was watching the football game that was going on behind us. My squad was down on the track turning cartwheels and yelling ourselves hoarse (and did I mention it was FREEZING????) and no one cared!!! I managed to sneak away and make my way up to Mom and Dad's seats.

"Plum, what are you doing here?" Mom asked, her teeth chattering. "You're supposed to be down there ch-ch-ch-cheering."

"I don't get it," I said. "No one is watching us. They're all watching the football game. We've been practicing routines for days just so we could come out here and die of cold while we cheer for a bunch of stupid smelly boys who keep running into each other?! What are we doing here, Mom?"

Mom got a funny look on her face. "Yes, indeed," she said softly. "What *are* we doing here?"

We were heading to the parking lot when the head cheerleader's mom blocked our way. "Where are you going?" she asked.

"We've got to go," Mom said. "Errr, Plum doesn't feel well."

I guess I wasn't that surprised Mom lied. She fibs all the time. She says sometimes you need to tell white lies to spare people's feelings or to avoid confrontation. Dad thinks that's a bunch of hooey. He's a Truther. I don't think he's ever told a lie in his life.

He leaned over Mom's shoulder and said, "That's not true. Plum feels fine—just a bit frozen—but otherwise fine. She's come to the realization that she's wasting her time—and our time—by being here and so we're leaving."

The woman sputtered something about personal responsibility and being part of a team and finishing what you start and blah, blah, blah. That's when Dad cut her off and said, "Do me a favor, would ya? Don't parent my kid and I won't parent yours."

And Mom said, "Excuse us, please. We're going to get some hot chocolate!"

After that one cold experience, I never tried cheerleading again.

My lack of interest for cheerleading and pep rallies in general must have been showing on my face, because that's when Frat Boy went crazy. Like, certifiable. Everyone stood on their feet and cheering loudly. They shook homemade signs and pom-poms on sticks. I wasn't standing, and Frat Boy took that as a personal affront. He started grabbing at me, trying to hoist me to my feet. Here's the thing, usually I'm not very stoked about being one of the thickest girls in my grade, but for once I was thrilled I outweighed this boy, because he couldn't get me to budge.

"Stand up! Show your pride!" he grunted, yanking my arms. "Get up, you … you … fat pink cow!"

I wanted to say, "Mcscuse me, bro? Did you call me a cow?! Oh hail no!"

You know how you can make fun of your family, but no one else can make fun of your family? Like, ever? That's how I feel about my size. *I* can say I'm fluffy or chubby or whatever, but NO ONE ELSE can say that about me! My body is off limits. No one gets to say a word about my figure. Not unless you want to see me go psycho. I have struggled with my weight since…well, since I was born probably. Mom says I just need to get a little taller, stretch out a bit. I don't think that's going to happen. I think I'm done growing. The only things still growing on me are my boobs and butt. I know what I look like. I'm not thrilled with it, but I'm learning to accept it and love it and I did not need this mollycoddled POS calling me a cow. What the hell, man? That kind of insult can give a girl a complex! It can make her have body issues! I'm a delicate fucking flower and I didn't want to hear anything more coming out of his soggy, fleshy mouth.

So, I stood up and I shoved Frat Boy.

I don't know why I did that. It was the third time in less than an hour that I reacted so unlike myself. I don't know what I was thinking exactly. I think the problem was that I *wasn't thinking*.

I just wanted some space to breathe. He was so close to me. He'd had pizza for lunch, and I could feel his hot onion breath on my face. I wanted his grubby mitts off me. His clammy hands kept twisting my arm, and his touch was grossing me out. It was like being handled by someone with hams for hands. I wanted his foul breath out of my face and his paunchy paws off me. I wanted him to step off and give me room and to shut his giant gaping maw. I wanted to check him a bit and let him know that calling me—or any other female—a cow was unacceptable and reprehensible. I wanted to send a warning shot across his bow.

All these things were rolling around in my brain. I was so agitated and frustrated I couldn't form a complete sentence or explain to him why he needed to move away from me. So, instead, I went straight into Toddler Mode and shoved him.

When I shoved him I didn't think about the fact that he wasn't even remotely ready to take a hit from someone who weighed as much as he did. Nor did I consider the fact we were fifteen rows up and standing at the top of an empty staircase. I probably should have thought of these things, at least a little bit, because

down,

down,

down he went.

I was horrified at first, but then it was kind of comical. His eyes opened really wide and his mouth made this perfect "O" as he flailed his arms wildly trying to keep his balance. But he couldn't fight physics. He went end over end with an audible "oof" each time he hit something, and he literally bounced over about three steps in the middle. He landed heavily on the gymnasium floor, sprawled out and crying for his mommy, right in Emberleigh's path. She didn't see him there because she was in The Zone. She had continued with her routine on the floor while I was fighting with Frat Boy in the stands and she'd missed the whole thing. Emberleigh was in the middle of a roundoff when she ran straight into Frat Boy and landed soundly on her butt. The whole gym erupted into laughs and jeers.

Emberleigh was shocked to see she was in a tangled pile with a blubbering boy and looked up to see where he'd come from. There was no question who was responsible. I was still standing at the top of the stairs with my arms extended in front of me. If looks could kill I would have died a horribly slow and painful death right there.

I was almost relieved when Mr. Mustache snatched my arm and marched me down to Principal Cutler's office. "Let's go, missy!"

Long story even longer: I can't go to school tomorrow and Mom and Dad are going to kill me when I tell them. I kind of wish Emberleigh HAD killed me.

Plum's Punch List:

1. Pep rallies
2. School pride
3. Pig-faced boys
4. Mustaches
5. Cheerleading

Friday

August 26

I'm in HUUUUGE trouble. Huge, I tell ya. I got suspended until Monday.

Mom and Dad are furious. Mom cried—of course. Dad yelled—of course. Pax snorted—of course.

Mom and Dad are punishing me with manual labor. They made me work all day! When I wasn't scrubbing toilets with a toothbrush, shining the rims on Dad's car with a toothbrush, or polishing Mom's diamond ring with a toothbrush (what is the deal with my parents demanding everything be cleaned with toothbrushes??!!), I was forced to spend that time reflecting on my actions.

Mom didn't think I was reflecting enough, so she told me to write an essay about who I think I am. After two hours of staring at a blank page, trying to write, all I came up with was "I yam what I yam."

Mom read the paper probably fifty times before she finally said through gritted teeth, "You're grounded until you're thirty, Plum."

"But that's impossible," I argued.

"Thirty-five!" Mom yelled. "Now, go to your room before I make it forty!"

Plum's Punch List:

1. Toothbrushes
2. Bogus essay assignments

Monday

August 29

Pax woke me up this morning. "Wakey-wakey, jailbird," he said, kicking the end of my bed.

I grumbled and rolled over. "What time is it?" One of the perks of being suspended and grounded is that you can totally sleep in. Mom was so sick of my face she actually preferred not to see me before noon.

"Six thirty," Pax said. "You get to go back to school today."

"Ugh." *Get to.* Ha. More like *have to.* I have decided I need to get into more fights at school. Maybe I could get myself expelled even, and then I'd have to be homeschooled.

"Look," Pax said. "It's not going to be so bad. Everyone is talking about the *incident.*" He made air quotes.

"The *incident?*"

"Yeah, that's what Cutler called it. He was like, 'There was an *incident* at the pep rally and we're all pulling for Malcolm to make a full recovery.'"

I sat up in bed and rubbed my eyes. "Who's Malcolm?"

"The kid whose ass you kicked," Pax said, grinning.

"Oh. Right."

"Anyway, there's a lot of chatter, but the good news is, you have a lot of people on your side. Malcolm's a douchebag."

"Yeah, I got that when we met."

"There's just kind of one little thing, though," Pax said. He rubbed the back of his neck, worrying.

"What? What's the little thing?" I asked.

"He's in remedial math *and* English classes."

"Great." I groaned. "So now I look like a bully who picks on slower kids?"

"Pretty much."

Sure enough, when I got to school Ollie filled me in. He told me Emberleigh and her coven of witches told everyone the insane girl with pink hair who Hulked out on a poor, defenseless boy with disabilities, breaking his leg and causing Emberleigh to bruise her tailbone in the process (she swears that's a real thing and that it's as painful as a broken leg, if not more so) is a danger to our school and a real threat to everyone. She and her mother even talked to the head of the school district to see if I can be sent to another high school.

"Wonderful," I sighed. "Just wonderful."

The bell rang. "You'd better get going, bruiser," Ollie said. "You can't get a detention on your first day back."

I kept my head down most of the day, only answering questions from the teachers when I absolutely had to. I ate lunch in the girls' room, avoiding public spaces as much as possible. At the end of the day I found several notes shoved in my locker. Most of them were illegible. I think they were positive, but who knows? One of the few I could read was written in large block letters. It said, "WTG! DOWN WITH THE EFFING PATRIARCHY." Another one called me a "Fat, flaming cow." A third one said, "You're the bravest person I've ever seen."

Wow. That one was a keeper. I was thinking I should get it framed or something.

After school I went to talk to Mom, but her door was shut. I thought maybe she was on a conference call or something, but then I heard Dad's voice too. He was home from work. Already? That was strange.

"Look, Lily, I'm under a lot of pressure right now," Dad said.

"And I'm not?" Mom said.

"Your pressure is different. Yours is self-imposed."

"I'm under pressure because your job isn't secure, Ben!" Mom said.

That part made me a little nervous.

"Well, maybe it's time for you to be the breadwinner," Dad said. "I've been carrying this family for years now. Maybe I'd like a break! It must be nice to sit around all day in pajamas and drinking tea while you flit about on the Internet."

"Is that what you really think I do all day?" Mom screeched.

"Hey," Dad's voice had softened. "I don't want to fight with you. I'm sorry. I'm just so damn miserable these days."

"Well, it's no picnic over here, either," Mom said. "Try dealing with your daughter, the queen of the misfits, and her shenanigans. I didn't get anything done while she was suspended."

Queen of the misfits? That's crazy, right? Plus, kettle meet pot, because Mom is the Queen queen of Dramatown.

"I know," Dad sighed.

"I know what would make us all happy again," Mom said.

"What?"

"We should move back to Jersey."

My heart skipped a beat.

"Lily, you know we can't do that."

"Why not?"

"You know why not. My job here might not be that secure, but it's still something. I can't move to Jersey without a job. We can't afford to move across the country again if the company isn't paying for it. We can't sell this house that fast. There are just too many reasons that we can't do it."

Mom sighed. "Well, then you're going to have to suck it up and make this job work."

"Do you think I don't know that?"

"I'm not sure what you know, Ben. It's three o'clock in the afternoon and you're standing in my office instead of yours. That doesn't look like sucking it up to me."

"We just need you to write more books. A book a year isn't going to do it. I ran some numbers last night—"

"You ran some numbers?" Mom asked, incredulous.

"Yeah. Listen, if you wrote between four and six books a year, I could quit my job. I could work for you. I could help you. I could do your marketing, run your social media, whatever you need me to do to free you up to write more. I could quit my job and work with you. We'd both spend all day in our PJs, drinking tea, and flitting on the Internet."

"If I just whip up between four and six books a year!" Mom yelled. "Are you kidding me? When do you think I have the time to do that? I haven't gotten anything done in weeks! I've spent the last month doing nothing but propping up our daughter. Trying to boost her confidence, help her fit in, get a friend or two. She is a full-time job, Ben!"

I wanted to push open the door and yell, "Me? A full-time job? You've been propping me up and boosting my confidence for the last month? Really? Because if that's true, then you suck at your job!" Was she even serious? Because everything—everything—has been about Mom since we'd arrived in Kansas. That is all she cared about. When she met Emberleigh and Mrs. Davidson, Mom made the drama all about her. *Mrs. Davidson thinks I peddle smut! Mrs. Davidson will turn everyone in town against me! Oh, and you too, Plum.* When I got suspended she freaked out that I would interfere with her deadlines. Not to mention she totally sided against me and let the school suspend me. Whatever happened to the mother who once told me, "If a boy ever puts his hands on you in any way that is unwanted you have my permission to kick him in the balls. I will defend your right to defend your body!" Where was that mother? Not in the office with me and Mr. Cutler when he handed out my punishment. She just nodded her head and said, "Thank you for not expelling her." She let me clean her shit with toothbrushes while she spent the whole time on the phone crying to my grandma about how hard it was for her! And now Dad is miserable at his job. MISERABLE. He hates his life and she tells him to suck it up, buttercup. Unbelievable!!

I thought about confronting her and giving her my two cents, but what would that accomplish? Mom would just cry and try to make me feel bad for attacking her or whatever, and Dad would add five more years to my grounding. I dug in my pocket and fished out the note from my locker. "You are the bravest person I've ever seen."

Ha! What does that person know? I'm not even brave enough to confront my own parents.

Plum's Punch List:

1. My mama's drama

Tuesday

August 30

Last night I got a text message. I was all, *Finally!* Because I thought maybe Kennedy was finally answering my billion and one messages. I snatched the phone and scrolled greedily. There was one message, and it was from a number I didn't recognize:

UR THE BRAVEST PERSON I'VE EVER SEEN. Followed by a ridiculous amount of emojis, including smiley face blowing kisses, four tacos, a farmer, a bunch of gold medals, a woman holding a blowtorch, and a flexing arm.

"What the hell?" I muttered.

WHO THIS? I typed.

SECRET ADMIRER

A secret admirer? Whoa. Instantly I imagined a super hot guy sitting in his room nervously texting me. Only hot guys are secret admirers, right?

Me: HOW DID U GET THIS #?

Secret Admirer: SCHOOL DIRECTORY.

Me: U KNOW ME?

Secret Admirer: PLUM PARRISH. THE PINK PUGILIST.

Holy shit. My new hot boyfriend was a wordsmith. I swooned. Literally.

Me: WHAT'S UR NAME?

Secret Admirer: Fadia.

Then I was like, *Wait. Whut? Isn't that a chick name?*

Me: UR GIRL?

Secret Admirer: YES!!!

I had so many questions, but I didn't know how to ask them appropriately:

1. Who was Fadia? The name sounded vaguely familiar, but I'd only been at SPHS for a couple of weeks and I'd barely met anyone.
2. Was I supposed to know who she was?
3. Had we already met and like an ass I'd completely forgotten already?
4. Was Fadia gay? Or was she just girl-crushing rather than like a full-on crush-crush?
5. If it was a full-on crush-crush did she know I was straight, or was she hoping this was going to go somewhere?
6. Was she a loony? Did she want to wear my skin like last year's Versace?

I tabled all my questions and decided to go with:

Me: COOL.

Fadia: I WATCH U, BUT IM NOT A STALKER.

Me: COOL. GOOD TO KNOW.

Fadia: U KICKED MALCOLM'S ASS. U TELL QUEEN BEE AND WANNABEES TO STICK IT. UR BADASS.

Okay, at that point I was convinced I was being punked. I crossed the hall to Pax's room because I was fairly certain he was behind this text exchange.

Pax put down the book he was reading. Side note: that right there convinced me he was in on it, because I've never seen Pax do anything with a book except kill spiders. "Hey, what's up?"

"Are you texting me weird stuff?" I asked.

"Weird stuff?"

"Yeah, like stuff to puff me up or something. Mom said that she's been spending a lot of time propping me up and making me feel better about myself. Are you in on her game?"

Pax scowled. "Of course not. That sounds like a waste of time. Why would you need propping?"

I shrugged. "I dunno. I guess because I'm sort of a mess."

"You're not a mess, Plum."

"I am! You said I was a lot to handle and I needed to fit in more."

Pax sighed heavily. "Are we doing this again? I already explained to you what I meant by that."

"No, I know. It's just that it's been really hard at school lately but now I'm getting these messages from someone and I'm leery."

Pax finally looked concerned. "What kind of messages are you getting? Nasty stuff? Are you getting cyberbullied?"

I shook my head. "No, just the opposite. I have a cyber fan."

"What is that?"

"Some chick who is telling me what a badass she thinks I am."

Pax smiled broadly. "Well, there you go. It's about time someone noticed."

"You swear it's not you or one of your bros playing games with me?"

Pax's face was serious. "I would never play that kind of game with you, Plum. You're my sister. That would be so uncool."

"I'm in no state for any nonsense. I'm barely holding it together as it is. I've got Cutler on my ass, Emberleigh and her posse breathing down my neck, and Malcolm working up a crocodile tear every time I see him. If someone is fucking with me, it will literally kill me."

"Let me see the messages." I handed my phone to Pax. "You don't know who this girl is?"

"No clue."

"Well, let's look in the school directory. There can't be that many Fadias, right?"

"True."

Pax pecked at the keyboard on his laptop and the directory appeared. It was alphabetical with a small thumbnail headshot next to each entry. "Here she is. Fadia Sayed. Ninth grader. Same as us."

I studied the picture of a somber girl with large eyes and a headscarf. "I know her! I saw her in the hallway when Emberleigh ran into her."

"See? There you go. This girl is for real."

"Huh. Who would've thought?"

Pax chortled. "Not me, that's for sure. You're definitely changing, Plum. It's like when you pushed Malcolm down the stairs you woke something up."

I smiled. "Yeah, watch out, world."

I texted Fadia. MEET ME AT MY LOCKER TOMORROW B4 SCHOOL.

She replied with eighteen thumbs up.

And just like that I had two friends.

Plum's Punch List:

1. Whoever made emojis, because that crap is annoying

Wednesday

August 31

As soon as I entered the school today, Mr. Cutler was there waiting for me. "Good morning, Plum," he said.

"Hey," I said, craning my neck to see if Fadia was waiting at my locker.

"Please come with me."

"Yeah, okay," I said. "I just need to drop this stuff at my locker." I didn't want to keep Fadia waiting.

"You can do that later. Right now you have an appointment."

Mr. Cutler deposited me in a cluttered office with inspirational posters covering the walls. ("If 'Plan A' doesn't work, you've got 25 more letters to try!" and "If opportunity doesn't knock, check to see if the doorbell is broken.") I was trying to text Fadia an update on my status when Mr. Mustache—the one who had forced me to go back to the pep rally—came in. Ugh! He was the one who caused the whole mess! If he had just let me skip out like I'd wanted, none of this would have happened. Malcolm's leg wouldn't be broken and Emberleigh's tailbone wouldn't be bruised (insert eye roll here) and I wouldn't be grounded until I'm thirty-five. I had nooooo desire to talk to that guy. I slumped down in my chair and gave him my very best scowl.

"Hello, Plum," Mr. Mustache said. I scowled harder (as if that were possible). "I said, 'Hello, Plum.' Polite people typically respond to a greeting."

I sighed heavily. "Hello, Mr. Mus—" It was so close! I stopped myself just in time. "Hey," I muttered.

"I'm Mr. Clarence. I'm your guidance counselor."

I didn't say anything. I mean, what are you supposed to say? "Yippee!" or "Like, who cares??" or how about "You've pretty much ruined my entire life. Thanks a bunch." I heard the first bell ring and I got kind of antsy. I was totally going to miss Fadia. I glanced at the door, eager to get going.

Mr. Clarence saw me. He must have thought I was worried about being tardy and getting in trouble or something. "Don't worry, Plum. I'll give you a hall pass. I want to have a discussion with you this morning."

Ohhhhhh grrrrrrrreeaaaaaat. A discussion. Just what I needed. Blergh.

Only, it wasn't really a discussion so much as a lecture. Mr. Clarence launched into a one-man show where he droned on and on about how he was once an outsider in high school too. (Teachers, they're just like us!) And how he didn't fit in and the kids called him "Pudgy." He talked about how he found football to be a great outlet for him. I rolled my eyes at that point, because honestly, what was he suggesting? That I join the football team? Not. Gonna. Happen. He said he could see I've got some "pent-up anger" and that I need an outlet for my emotions or else it's going to be a "very long year" for me at Sunset Pines.

I wanted to argue that I'm not angry, I am just irritated—perpetually perturbed, if you will. There's a difference. Angry implies I want to burn things down or hurt someone. Irritated is just fed up, vexed, galled, or exasperated with what's going on around me. I'm not angry. I don't want to hurt people ... well, except maybe for Malcolm. He was an exception. But when I pushed him I didn't *intend* to hurt him—it was a joyous happenstance. Plus, I am still not convinced his leg is even broken. Mr. Clarence said it was a fractured ankle. Malcolm seems the type to be a crybaby who would probably fake that fractured ankle for the attention. He needs to nut up, because really, isn't a fracture just a bad sprain? Ollie told me Malcolm doesn't have a cast or anything. And don't even get me started on Emberleigh's bruised tailbone. If you ask me, I'd say she's been looking for an excuse for her entire life to sit on a pillow 24/7! You're welcome, Emberleigh.

Then Mr. Clarence talked about finding your tribe and how important it is to have a group of friends who really get you and understand you.

"I had a group like that," I said. "At my old school."

Mr. Clarence smiled kindly. "Yes, well, you'll need a new tribe here, Plum."

I snorted. "That's a lot easier said than done, you know."

"I understand. How did you find your tribe at your old school?" he asked.

"We all met in kindergarten."

"Okay, but you can't be friends with everyone from kindergarten. You must have had one or two close friends. What did you have in common?"

"French Club."

"Oh. Hmm." Mr. Clarence kind of pet his mustache while he thought. (Ewww.) "We have Spanish Club."

"I know," I said. SPHS doesn't have French Club. There isn't even a French teacher—only Spanish.

"Not interested in Spanish, huh?"

I hoped my sneer spoke for itself.

"So, French is kind of your jam, huh?" he said.

My jam. Yeah. He really said that. I was sooooooo embarrassed for him. I was ready to go silent and shut down completely, but I could see his face was kind and he was really trying to help me—even if he was going about it in a totally awkward way. He was trying more than anyone else at SPHS had so far. Mr. Cutler had just dumped me on Emberleigh, easily the last person anyone in their right mind would think could be my friend. None of my teachers had learned my name yet. One calls me Paige (close) and another one calls me Trish (yeah, I have no idea either). The rest call me the Girl With the Pink Hair. "What is the answer? Yes, you, Girl With the Pink Hair. What is 'X'?"

I could see Mr. Clarence really wanted to help me. I wondered if maybe I should let him? It wasn't like I could really talk to my parents these days. Between Dad's craptastic job and Mom's nonstop work/moving/child-rearing stress, they were in their own world of hurt. Mr. Clarence might have missed the mark with all the football team nonsense, but at least he he was trying. I appreciated his effort. It was nice to have someone who cared.

That's when I developed a severe case of verbal diarrhea. I didn't mean to, but there was something about Mr. Clarence that made me want to share all of my feelings. I just dumped it all on him. So. Much. Word. Vomit. I told him that Madame O'Malley and French Club pretty much saved my life in sixth grade. That was the year Pax officially became cool and left me in the dust. The writing had been on the wall for a few years, but sixth grade was when the lines were drawn and Pax was welcomed into the arms of the elite and I was banished to Weirdo Town. Actually, that's not true, Weirdo Town didn't even want me. I was pretty much on my own. I had no people. I didn't know what to do without my twin, so I was sort of floundering. I was a decent French student and Madame O'Malley invited me to join the French Club. That's where I met Kennedy and we became good friends. We'd known one another since preschool, but it wasn't until we realized our shared love of *Français* that we became BFFs. Mr. Clarence nodded and took a few notes, but I didn't stop there, I kept going. I explained that Madame O'Malley also taught high school French and she'd suggested Kennedy and I be co-leaders of the high school French Club this year. Sure, no one else had wanted the job, but it was still a huge honor to be asked. The high school French Club goes to Montreal for a long weekend in the spring, and Kennedy and I were planning the coolest trip ever. It was going to be epic and we'd go down in history as the greatest French Club co-leaders. But now I was devastated because I couldn't go to Montreal and because Kennedy hadn't returned any of the eighty-two emails and texts (100 percent accurate number, I added them up last night) I'd sent her. I should have stopped there. That was enough. But I didn't. I told Mr. Clarence about Emberleigh and how mean she's been to me since she met me. How she ditched me at lunch and forced me to eat in the girls' bathroom. I told him about Malcolm's face as he fell down the bleachers and how I felt sorry but not sorry as he tumbled ass over teakettle. I told him about Mrs. Davidson's meeting with the superintendent and trying to get me transferred to a different school. I was upset because I'm not a huge fan of SPHS, but I sure as hell didn't want to try another school! I also told him about what Mrs. Davidson said to my mom. That's when Mr.

Clarence held up a hand and finally spoke.

"Plum, are you embarrassed by what your mom does for a living?" he asked.

"It's her dream," I squeaked.

He shook his head. "That wasn't my question. I want to know if you're embarrassed by your mother."

Was I embarrassed that my mom wrote books about couples getting freaky? Was I embarrassed that she speaks louder than any other mother I know and uses words like "menses" and "labia" instead of "period" and "vagina"? Was I embarrassed she thinks nothing of showing up at school in her pajamas so she can drop off the lunch I left on the counter? Was I embarrassed she still insists on tucking me into bed each night and kissing me—on the lips? Was I embarrassed she curses all the time, even when she's writing a shopping list? Seriously. Once I found a list that said:

1. Bananas
2. Shitty bread that Ben likes
3. Chicken breasts

I liked Mr. Clarence and I wanted to be honest, but who knows what he'd do with the truth if I blurted out, "Yes! A thousand times yes I am embarrassed by my mother!"? Sometimes you have to tell a white lie to spare someone's feelings or to avoid a confrontation. I answered as truthfully as I could. "Isn't every ninth grader embarrassed by their mother?"

"Fair enough," he replied.

By the time he released me, the halls were completely empty. I went to my locker, half hoping Fadia would be there, but of course she wasn't.

I texted her.

SORRY I MISSED U THIS AM. GOT YANKED INTO COUNSELOR OFFICE. WANT TO MEET FOR LUNCH?

She replied instantly. OF COURSE!!!!

Fadia was waiting for me outside the lunchroom. When I saw her, I became nervous. I wasn't sure what I'd say to her. "Be cool," I muttered.

I walked up to her. She was leaning against the wall, scrolling through her phone. "Hey," I said, nudging her.

She looked up from the screen and pulled an earbud out. "Hey," she said, grinning broadly.

I stood there awkwardly, not sure what to do. Should I hug her or something? "So…" I said.

"So," she replied.

"We should eat, yeah?"

"Totally," she said.

"Okay."

We entered the lunchroom and I saw Ollie had a table saved for us. I'd filled him in on the whole Fadia situation during art class, so he was completely up to speed when we sat down.

"Hi, I'm Ollie," he said, extending his hand to Fadia.

"Hello! Fadia," she said, shaking his hand.

I should have shaken her hand! That's what normal people do when they meet for the first time. Duh! Better late than never. I stuck out my hand. "I'm Plum."

Fadia giggled and said, "Of course you are."

We sat in silence for what seemed like an hour, but that's impossible since lunch is only twenty minutes. A few things struck me as interesting slash strange:

1. Fadia brought PB&J from home. I don't know what I thought she'd eat for lunch, but PB&J was not on my short list. For some reason I was thinking lamb-something.

2. Fadia cusses. A LOT. That girl could teach Mom some new words. I guess I assumed that with the headscarf and everything she must be fairly religious and devout, but then she drops F-bombs like I say "like."

3. Fadia is funny.

I really didn't say much. I was sort of tongue-tied and I didn't want to ask an offensive question or anything, but Ollie wasn't afraid. He dove right in with, "Do you have hair under there?" he asked, nodding at Fadia's headscarf.

"Ollie!" I screeched.

Fadia smiled. "Tons of hair."

"You must save a lot of money on hairspray, huh?" Ollie asked.

"Whatever I save I spend on new scarves," Fadia said.

"Ahh, of course." Ollie nodded. "Those can't be cheap."

"I don't like the cheap ones," Fadia said. "I'm high maintenance."

"Do you have a boyfriend?" Ollie asked.

"Do you?" Fadia countered.

"Two," Ollie said, grinning. "High maintenance and sassy!"

"Have you ever had a girlfriend?" Fadia asked.

"Have you?" Ollie asked.

"Two." Fadia said.

Ollie choked on his juice. "Vixen!"

"Wait. Really?" I asked.

Fadia laughed. "I'm kidding. Totally kidding. No boyfriends or girlfriends."

Their banter went on like that for the rest of lunch. I found out Fadia is the middle daughter of five girls. She said she's the stereotypical middle child: feels misunderstood, needs more attention from her parents, rebels, etc., etc.

"Meh." Ollie waved his hand dismissively. "Every fifteen-year-old feels that way, not just you middle children."

She's Muslim (which I'd already guessed), but she's kind of a black sheep. She's not allowed to talk to boys—ever, but it doesn't stop her. She doesn't like to go to the mosque very much and she's obsessed with all things bacon, which she eats on the sly. "I honestly don't know which would be worse, if my dad caught me with a boy or a BLT," she said. She was born and raised in Kansas and hasn't traveled anywhere except to California every two years to visit her cousins who live there.

"My dad would have a shit fit if he knew I was having lunch with you," she told Ollie.

"Even though I don't dig your particular brand of chili?" Ollie asked.

Fadia thought. "Excellent question, but knowing my dad he'd be sure that my feminine wiles could turn you straight."

Ollie laughed bitterly. "And my daddy says he has nothing in common with *Mooslims*. Ha!"

"Oh, I bet those two narrow minds could find a lot more in common if they just tried. It's amazing how mutual dislike can bring two people together," Fadia said. Suddenly she turned to me. "Speaking of mutual dislike…"

"Emberleigh," I said.

"Mean Girl Barbie and her friends have no idea what to do with you, Plum Parrish," Fadia crowed.

I frowned. "What do you mean?"

"Don't you see? You threaten them."

"Me? How?"

"By simply being you. There is something about you that gets under Emberleigh's skin. I think part of is it that you just DGAF," Fadia said, pointing a finger at me.

Don't tell Fadia, but I *do* GAF. "That's not true at all," I said. "It's Ollie who has no f—cares—left to give."

Ollie mocked surprise. "Baby, please, you were the one who taught me."

Fadia nodded. "You went to a pep rally and read a book. A book! Who does that? Sure, there are people sitting there bored out of their minds and wishing they could be anywhere but there, but no one has the audacity to pull out a book and ignore Emberleigh and the football team and all the other quote unquote *leaders* of this school. No, they sit there and clap like the mindless automatons they are. And then when Malcolm told you to get on your feet and cheer. Cheer, little monkey! Scream, little monkey! Do what you're told, little monkey! You told him, essentially, to eat you."

Ollie turned a little green. "Eww."

"You stood your ground, literally, and showed him he could not mess with you," Fadia continued, ignoring Ollie. "But then when you stuck up for me. That's when I knew, Plum."

"You knew what?" I asked.

"I knew that you were my people. You and Ollie. You two have brought something I haven't seen in a long time."

"What's that?" Ollie asked. "Fashion sense? It's fashion, isn't it? News flash, captain of the wrestling team, bolo ties are not ties."

"No!" Fadia said. "You two brought some fresh goddamn air into this place. Finally I have some hope that life might be better than this rat maze where I spend three-quarters of my life trying to find the cheese all while yelling into a black hole: 'This can't be all there is!'"

I shrugged. I didn't know what to say. Sure I missed my school in New Jersey, but there were dillholes and bitches there, too. Nowhere was perfect. As far as I could tell, there would always be Emberleighs making our lives difficult while we all screamed into black holes. Look at Mom and Mrs. Davidson. "The world pretty much sucks for anyone who isn't a lemming," I said.

"True, but now I have some allies. I have some people on my side who are woke!" Fadia said, grabbing me by the arm. "You guys aren't going to follow along mindlessly while everyone around jumps off a cliff because Queen Emberleigh said they should. That's all I'm saying. Your eyes are open and so are mine. There's strength in numbers."

I let Fadia's words sink in. She was right. I might not feel 100 percent comfortable speaking up against Emberleigh, but I was doing it. I wasn't letting people like her or Malcolm push me around and make me do things I didn't want to do. I was asserting myself and (probably to Mr. Clarence's chagrin) I was asserting myself more and more every day. Between Mom's endless mantra of "You do you, Plum" and Pax's kick in the butt forcing me to own my "a lot-ness," I *was* changing. I was evolving and becoming more confident in my voice and more comfortable in my skin.

The bell rang, ending lunch. "Stay you, Plum," Fadia said, grabbing the trash from our table.

"Umm, yeah, okay," I mumbled.

Fadia grabbed my arm again. "The word of the day is 'resist.' All you have to do is resist, Plum. Don't fall for their shite. Don't get dragged into their petty arguments about who wore it best or discussions about lipgloss or football stats. There is more to life than high school."

"A-freaking-men," Ollie said.

"You're a badass, Plum Parrish. Remember that!"

"Hell yeah, I'm a badass!" I lied.

Plum's Punch List:

1. Spanish Club
2. Middle-age people who say "jam" and they're not talking about toast
3. White lies

Friday

September 2

And just like that, Labor Day weekend is upon us. On the one hand, a long weekend sounds *ah-may-zing*, but on the other hand, Pax got invited to a friend's lake house, and so I am on my own, which is going to be uber boring. I mean, it's not like he's terrific company, but at least he's *some* company, y'know? I was actually surprised Mom and Dad said Pax could go. Normally Mom is a helicopter mom of mammoth proportions and doesn't like to let us out of her sight. I am shocked she is letting Pax spend the weekend with parents she's barely met *and* surrounded by water. I was sort of jealous he was going somewhere fun, but then I saw the list of rules she made for him. It was ridiculous:

1. *Call me once you arrive safely at the house. (Actually, call me every day.)*
2. *Go to bed at a decent hour—10 PM is late enough!*
3. *Remember your manners—always use please and thank you, you weren't raised in a barn.*
4. *Remember our rules and expectations for you. We might not be with you, but we're WITH you and you are a reflection of Dad and me— make us proud.*
5. *Make good choices—always ask yourself, "Would Mom approve?"*

6. *Apply sunscreen every two hours. Melanoma is a killer!*
7. *Wear a life jacket at ALL TIMES (not only babies drown).*
8. *Don't eat peanuts. EVER EVER EVER EVER!*

Okay, so the peanuts thing is so left field, because neither of us have a peanut allergy. But Mom has always been afraid we might develop an allergy late in life and so she doesn't want us to ever eat a peanut unless she's close by with her EpiPen. Yes, she has an EpiPen. I have no idea where she got one since NONE of our family has life-threatening allergies that would require a doctor to write a prescription for such a thing. But leave it to Mom to figure out a way to get one...or six of them.

Blergh. School has only been out for two hours and I am already bored out of my mind.

Even Ollie is gone for the weekend. He went out of town for a family wedding or something. I must admit, I kind of tuned him out. It was a boring story about people I neither knew nor cared about and I was jealous everyone except me had big plans for the holiday weekend, so I quit listening as soon as he said, "I'll be gone for Labor Day weekend." I think he went to Ohio? Or Idaho? I dunno, maybe Iowa? All I know is that he is somewhere having fun without me.

#whatever

I am positive every kid at SPHS has a lake house or they were invited to one for the weekend. What's so great about lake houses anyway? I bet they're musty and full of spiders. And who wants to go waterskiing and sunbathing on a boat? That sounds terribly hot, and I'm way too pale to be out in the sun for very long. There isn't enough sunblock on the planet to prevent me from burning to a crisp. Plus, I get seasick if the boat is too small. And let's not forget fishing. Ugh. As if. I have no desire to touch a slimy, smelly fish! Nope, spending the weekend at a lake house sounds horrible. On second thought, I am so glad no one invited me.

Oh please! You know I'm lying, right?

I've never spent a night in a lake house or waterskied or fished before, and I would jump through hoops of fire for the opportunity to be invited to try any of those things. I could never say this out loud, though. Ollie would be horrified, and Pax would just make fun of me. So, I'll spend all weekend in my room scowling and pretending like I'm exactly where I want to be.

Mom didn't blubber when the minivan containing Pax and three other boys from the basketball team drove off, but she did grip me tightly and whisper, "At least I've still got you, Plum."

Greeeeaaaat. Just what you want to be: your mom's bestie.

Guess what Mom suggested we do?

If you said mani-pedis, you would be correct. *Le sigh.*

It is going to be a loooooong weekend.

Plum's Punch List:

1. Lake houses I'm not invited to
2. Out-of-town weddings
3. Mani-pedis!!!!!!!!!!!

Saturday
September 2

By this afternoon I was losing my mind from sheer boredom. I was researching whether or not people can go insane from lack of stimulation. Turns out, you totally can. It's a form of torture! I am being tortured!

I don't know why adults get all excited about three-day weekends. They always get stoked about staying home and doing yard work and stuff. Like Dad. He has spent all morning in the yard spreading mulch. Are you kidding me?? How was that better than working? I would rather spend fifteen hours stuck in a cubicle doing data entry before I'd get excited about spreading mulch.

I could tell he was going to ask me to come out and help him, so I made a calculated move: I interrupted Mom's writing time. It was risky, but I was willing to take the chance. See, Mom makes this big deal that if her office door is closed, she's "at work" and we're not to interrupt her, and if you do she will freak the freak out on you, but I had to do it. Dad was going to make me do yard work! I decided I could handle the wrath of Mom, plus, I had a plan.

"Hey, Mom," I said, pushing open the door.

Mom quickly x'd the boxes on the open windows on her computer. I glimpsed her Facebook page and a shoe site before they disappeared. "Plum! You can't just burst in here. I'm working!"

I looked at her computer. She'd missed a tab, so a site that appeared to sell only granny panties was still open.

When she saw me looking, she x'd that one too. "It's research!" she said.

"Uh-huh," I said. I really didn't care what Mom was doing and frankly, I've been in charge of washing the laundry long enough to know that it would do her a world of good to invest in some new undies. No one looks and feels their best in holey underwear. The woman calls herself Lacy Drawers, for goodness' sake, she should buy herself some lacy drawers! "I wanted to see if you wanted to take a break."

Mom shook her head. "Oh, I can't. I'm very busy. Why don't you go watch TV?"

"I'm lonely," I said, pouting. Pouting usually softens up Mom.

"Oh, Plum," Mom sighed. "Can't you call Ollie and see what he's up to?"

"He's gone away this weekend. Maybe Iowa? I can't remember."

Mom nodded. "What about that new friend of yours? Nadia?"

"Fadia."

"Right. What about her? I could drop you both off at the movies or something."

"She's busy this weekend. She has family in town." I didn't tell Mom that Fadia had invited me to dinner at her house. I'd told Fadia I was busy. I don't know why I said that exactly. Partly because I wanted her to think I had plans already. That dumb website suggested it.

37. Never take your first offer. Popular people have full calendars! Always be busy and then you can "cancel" or "rearrange your schedule" if you decide a soiree is worth your time.

The other reason I didn't want to go was because I don't know Fadia that well yet. We have a lot in common, but we're also so very different. What if I didn't like the food they served? What if I did something to insult her family? Was I supposed to wear a scarf on my head, too? Would they speak English, or would I be forced to sit there and try to understand what was being said about me? As you can see, my anxiety is high, thus the need to skip.

"What about Dad?"

No! I couldn't let her suggest I hang out with Dad. It was time. I had to make my move before I ended up on wheelbarrow duty. I shrugged. "I don't know what he's doing. Besides, I wanted to hang out with you."

Mom looked pleased. "With me? You did?"

"Yeah. I thought maybe you could take a much-deserved break and we could go and get mani-pedis."

"Mani-pedis? Really?" I think Mom had her computer shut down and was waiting for me in the van in less than thirty seconds.

I realize mani-pedis aren't my jam (as Mr. Clarence would say), but anything is better than yard work with Dad.

We were pulling out of the driveway when Dad flagged us down. "You girls going somewhere?" he asked, wiping the sweat off his brow. "I could use some help out here."

"No can do," Mom said. "Plum wants to go get mani-pedis!"

Dad looked surprised. "You do, Plum?"

"Totally," I said.

"All right, well, you two have fun. Maybe you'll help me when you get back?" Dad asked.

"I doubt it," Mom said.

Dad groaned. "Come on, Lily."

"I'm just being honest."

"Do you know what a manicure costs?" I asked. "We'd be wasting your money if we came home and ruined our manicures working in the yard."

Mom nodded vigorously. "Besides," she said. "I like to see you all sweaty and dirty."

Dad smiled and wagged his eyebrows. "Yeah, you do."

I threw up a little bit in my mouth. "Can we go now, please?"

"See ya, babe!" Mom said, rolling up her window.

"We should also try and find a new hairstylist today," I said, checking my roots in the side mirror.

"And get lunch," Mom said.

"And hit the bookstore."

"And I want to look at shoes," Mom added. "And underwear."

"Even if we wanted to, I don't think we're going to be back in time to help Dad. He'll probably be finished before us."

"Fingers crossed," Mom said.

Plum's Punch List:

1. Three-day weekends
2. Yard work
3. I'm not going to say mani-pedi this time, because Mom and I actually had fun—God, I must really be bored!!

Sunday

September 4

I've been waiting forever for Mom to find a new stylist. We tried yesterday, but no dice. She says finding a new stylist is like finding a boyfriend. You have to really get in there and get to know them. Figure out how they "tick."

"Your hair is incredibly important," Mom said. "It's one of the first things people see when they meet you. Can you imagine if you had a bad haircut?"

YES!!! However, that has never been a concern before now. Hellooooo! I've had bad haircuts my whole life until the last one, and Mom's had countless bad haircuts. There was the time she rocked that suburban mom-do where it's a waterfall in the front, but spiky in the back. I swear I cut myself once just hugging her. Her hair drew blood. Another time she wanted bangs like some movie star she saw in a magazine and when she got home from the salon she didn't like them. She didn't think they looked like the celebrity's bangs. More like, *she* didn't look like the celebrity. Forget the fact the actress she was copying was fifteen years younger, seventy pounds lighter, and gorgeous. Instead, Mom convinced herself the problem was the bangs were uneven, so she took a pair of scissors to them. I don't know if they were uneven before she started hacking on them, but they were definitely uneven by the time she was finished.

I had a couple inches of roots showing and I was tired of waiting for Mom. It was time to take matters into my own hands. I decided the color was more upsetting than the cut. I could live with my shaggy hair, but I couldn't stand my roots anymore. Plus, the color has completely faded out to a horrible shade of orange-tinged sand. There was no way I could go back to school with that hair. Problem was I didn't have enough money to pay a stylist to color my hair, but a quick online search showed I could easily purchase the necessary materials for a home dye job for a fraction of the price.

I didn't think Mom would be down with my plan, and I had no way to get to the store. This was a job for Dad.

I convinced him to take a break from trimming trees and take me the drugstore. It wasn't hard at all. I swear, parents are such suckers for a teenager who says she wants to spend time with them. Dad even suggested we go see a movie or something. I was like, "Easy, killer. I barely know you. Let's take this slow, shall we? I just need a ride to Target."

We hit the Starbucks and scored a couple of pumpkin spice lattes. The barista told me that the PSL is not officially on the menu yet for the season, but that if you know to ask, they'll make you one special. I even convinced Dad to try one. He was worried his man card would be revoked just for ordering it. He loved it. Of course he did! What's not to love?

I know what you're thinking. You think I'm basic because I like PSLs. Well, you know what? If loving PSLs is wrong, then I don't want to be right. Yes, it was 90 degrees and I was in shorts, but I was so ready to kick off the PSL season. Just drinking that hot cup of awesome made me think of slouchy sweaters and leggings and Uggs and...OMG, I AM BASIC!

No way! I refuse to believe I'm basic. "You do you, Plum" as Mom would say. Exactly! I will do me!

Okay, back to my story. I left Dad in the Starbucks while I went to find the supplies I needed. He was exhausted and so grateful to be in air-conditioning that he didn't even argue when I suggested he stay behind. He took a seat gratefully and found a discarded newspaper. "Take your time," he urged, sipping his drink. "I might get another one of these."

Watch out, world! Tomorrow I shall have my beautiful pink tresses back!

Plum's Punch List:

1. NONE. It's PSL season, britches!

Monday

September 5

You might recall yesterday when I was all perturbed about Mom's sloth-like pace in finding me a stylist and so I took matters into my own (inexperienced) hands? Well, let's just say we've always known that math isn't one of my strong suits and now we can safely add chemistry to that list. Or telling time!

Let me start from the beginning. The horrible, horrible beginning.

Okay, so, my natural hair color is brown and for the pink to show up, I knew I needed to bleach it blond first. I bought some bleach and followed the directions on the package. I thought, *How hard can this be?* Umm ... pretty fracking hard, apparently!

So, you put it on your hair and then you're supposed to set a timer, but I didn't, because I'm a tool. I thought, *I can watch the clock. I'm not an idiot.* After twenty minutes you're supposed to check every ten minutes to see how light your hair is getting. Once it's as light as you want it, you rinse. The problem was I didn't like how fast the pink faded last time and all the articles I read online said the lighter or more bleached-out base you had to begin with, the better for your color. It would be brighter and more vibrant and longer-lasting. That's what I wanted.

I think I left the bleach on for an hour...or so. Thereabouts. I think. Now do you see the problem? I'm actually not sure since I didn't set a timer. I glanced at the clock when I first put the bleach on, but then I forgot what time I started. So when it felt like twenty minutes, I started checking every ten minutes. But after two (I think?) sets of additional ten minutes I got super confused. I couldn't remember if that was one ten-minute set or two ten-minute sets and since I'd forgotten what time I'd started, I really had no idea how long the bleach had been on my hair. I was utterly confused, but I figured I'd start keeping track right then, which was hard because some text messages came in from Fadia and I lost track of time looking at the funny cat videos she sent me. Basically, it was a total cluster. That's when I decided I'd just watch my hair and then I'd *know* when I hit my desired color. I thought, *I have eyes. I know what blond hair looks like.* I didn't need a timer to tell me what color my hair was. I threw caution (and my brains) to the wind and checked my head whenever it *felt* like ten minutes had passed. Each time I wasn't satisfied. I wanted to go lighter! I didn't know how long I'd go, but ultimately the decision was made for me.

Long story even longer, I decided I'd gone light enough when my head started burning.

At first it was a little tingle. I was like, "Hmm, that's kind of irritating, huh?" Then the tingling got a bit more painful. Kind of a pokey pain. Like someone was poking something sharp at me. "Ow!" I said. Next up was the feeling you get when you get a bad sunburn. I had a strong desire to rub aloe vera on my scalp. I was just beginning to investigate the discomfort when suddenly it felt like my head was on fire. I half expected to see flames shooting from my head. I was running around my bathroom screaming, "Make it stop! Make it stop!" and then I realized I was the one who had to make it stop. DUH!!

I jumped in the shower, hoping that was the right remedy, because I didn't know what else to do. I rinsed my hair and immediately the burning sensation dissipated. I felt quite proud of myself for solving my problem.

I got out of the shower and I was immediately greeted by the most amazing white-blond hair I've ever seen. Sure, my scalp felt like it was still smoking in places, but the color!! It was super cool, but freaky all at the same time. (It was probably a good thing I liked how it looks, because…well, we'll get to that part.)

So, now I've got this white-blond hair and I want to dye it pink, right? The directions said my hair needs to be dry before I apply the pink, but no blow-dryer allowed—that could damage the hair. So I wrapped my head in a towel and sat down to sketch a little and troll Emberleigh's Insta (she's at the lake, of course). About an hour later I was sick of seeing duck-face photos and PSLs (apparently I wasn't the only one who got the supersecret memo they're available early) and I decided to check my hair and see if it was dry yet.

I yanked off the towel and I felt something funny, like my hair was caught in the towel or something, but I didn't think much of it. Instead I flipped my head over and used the towel to dry my hair by rubbing it vigorously. Imagine my surprise when huge chunks of white-blond hair fell onto the floor at my feet.

HUGE CHUNKS.

It took me a full ten seconds to understand what I was seeing. At first I was like, "What is this blond fluffy stuff on the floor? Is that lint from the towel?"

Yeah, LINT. As if lint has ever looked like huge chunks of white-blond hair!!

My scalp was still sensitive and I reached up to gently rub a spot that was irritating me and when I touched bare skin that's when it all came together.

I'm pretty sure Mom and Dad thought I was being brutally murdered when they heard my screams. They came running up the stairs screaming themselves. "What? What is it? PLUM!???" Mom yelled, terrified. She burst through my door ready to fight off an attacker.

"I'm coming!" Dad flew in wielding garden shears.

"My hair!" I sobbed, holding up the HUGE CHUNKS.

TL;DR: Mom found me a stylist and now I have a white-blond crew cut with a couple of shiny red bald spots. When we stopped for consolation PSLs on the way home, the barista called me "sir." So this is my life now.

Plum's Punch List:

1. I can't even right now. I have to flee the country.

Tuesday
September 6

Pax survived the weekend—but just barely.

Seriously.

Turns out he IS allergic to bee stings. Who knew? Mom, of course, says she's always suspected, but our pediatrician would never believe her. Now she's convinced I'm allergic too, since we're twins. She's ordered more EpiPens. Soon we each will have one with our own personalized cases to carry them in—yeah, personalized EpiPen carrying cases are a real thing. She says we must carry our *ah-dor-able* personalized cases with us at all times in case a rogue bee stings us when she's not around to save our lives. I didn't argue with her since she was in a fragile state, but me carrying a personalized EpiPen case is NEVER GOING TO HAPPEN. I'll take my chances with the bees.

Here's how Pax almost died: he and his friends were told to clean the dock. He said since this was the first weekend the lake house was open after winter, the weekend consisted of more cleaning and fixing stuff than waterskiing and fishing. He never wants to own a lake house. The boys found a giant beehive attached to the ceiling of the dock and instead of getting help removing it, one of his Neanderthal friends had the bright idea to hit the hive with an oar and knock it into the lake. Yeah. It didn't go well for any of them.

I can only imagine how that conversation went:

Neanderthal 1: Me hit beehive with stick!

Neanderthal 2: No! ME hit beehive with stick!

Neanderthal 1: Okay, hit together. One … two … what come next?

Pax: Three! ARGH!!!!!!!

Pax got stung like fifty times or something insane like that. I thought my hair looked bad, but Pax looked way worse than me. He is so swollen, he looks like the Michelin Man. The boys ended up in some Podunk lake town ER, so while I was getting my head buzzed, Dad went to pick up Pax and bring him back to civilization where they could actually treat him with drugs made in this century. Poor Pax, not only does he look and feel terrible, he'll never get to leave our house again. I'll be surprised if Mom allows him go to college in four years. She still won't be ready to let him out of her sight.

He stayed home from school today, so SPHS felt even lonelier without him there. We don't hang out much, but it's still comforting to know my brother is close by. It was my first time being at school without him. Ollie was still out of town too. Probably just as well. I shudder to think what he's going to say about my new do. He might actually have a heart attack when he sees what I've done. I'm not ready for that conversation.

At least I have Fadia, I thought. I texted her to see if we could meet for lunch, but she said she had a club meeting during lunch.

Me: LUNCH?

Fadia: CAN'T. ROBOTIX TEAM MTG. U CAN COME IF U WANT.

Me: ROBOTICS? NO THX. EVEN I'M NOT THAT NERDY.

Fadia: NVMND, THEY SAID U CAN'T COME.

Me: RU SRS? WTF?

Fadia: NOPE. SAID UR HAIR IS TOO FKCD UP. HAHA. J/K.

Me: DAMN, U ROBOT DORKS R MEAN.

Fadia: IKR? C IF EMBERLEIGH WILL EAT W/U.

Me: SHE'S SAVING ME A SPOT.

Fadia: THOT SO. U 2 R BFFS 4 EVA. SAVE SUM MUSHY PEAS 4 ME.

Without Fadia or Ollie around, I spent another scintillating lunch hour in the girls' bathroom. It wasn't so bad. I finished my homework at least.

After lunch I was wandering the halls with my gaze fixed firmly on my

Chucks, because I'm not crazy about looking people in the eye—especially people who, thanks to Emberleigh, think I'm a loose cannon or whatever—when Mr. Clarence called my name.

"Plum!" he said, waving me over to the doorway where he was standing. "I want you to meet someone."

I threaded my way through a wall of upperclassmen and saw Mr. Clarence was standing beside Mr. Candy Crush—the teacher who told Mom well-rounded kids don't do well in his extracurricular activities. If he remembered me, his face didn't show it.

"Plum, this is Mr. Goodson. He's in charge of a number of our special clubs, including Spanish Club."

"I don't want to be in Spanish Club," I said, probably a bit more rudely than I meant to, but seriously, enough already with trying to get me to join the freaking Spanish Club! I guess I shouldn't complain too much, at least he'd moved away from football.

Mr. Clarence shook his head. "No, no. I was talking to Mr. Goodson about starting a French Club."

"But we don't even have French class here," I said, totally confused.

That's when Mr. Goodson finally spoke. "We don't have French Club because we don't have a French class. We don't have a French class because there hasn't been enough interest." Then he told me I needed to start a petition. Mr. Goodson's voice was the kind of voice that makes me want to put my fingers in my ears to drown it out. He has this nasally, high-pitched voice that instantly makes you want to hurt someone. I was fighting the urge to stick my fingers in my ears or punch someone when I heard him say, "You need to get 250 signatures from SPHS students saying they're interested in having French class."

"Two hundred and fifty?" I asked.

"Yes, then you take that petition to the school board and then they get to decide if there's enough money in the budget to hire a French teacher. If there is, then they'll hire a teacher," Mr. Goodson said. He held up a finger. "But at least one hundred students must sign up for French just to keep Madame Whomever in business. If the attendance drops below one hundred, Madame Whomever gets fired."

"But," Mr. Clarence said, "if French class sticks, then Madame—or Monsieur—Whomever can start French Club, correct?"

"Correct," Mr. Goodson said.

Mr. Clarence raised his eyebrows and said, "See? Easy peasy, right, Plum?"

Easy peasy???? Was he kidding me???? I don't know anyone except my brother, Ollie, and Fadia. Who was going to sign this petition? Two hundred and fifty kids was a quarter of the school. I would have to approach 250 kids and ask them to do me (a perfect stranger) a favor and sign a random petition. Actually, statistically that wouldn't work. There was no way that all 250 kids I approached would sign my petition. I'd probably have to talk to 500 kids just to get my 250 signatures. It would never work. I still haven't spoken to the girl who has the locker next to mine. I see her multiple times a day, several days a week and I can't even muster a "Hello," let alone a "Hi, would you please sign my petition for French class and then sign up to take French class so that we can create French Club and go to Montreal? Kthanxbai." ACK!!!! How was this going to work?

I might as well forget French Club, I thought. *C'est impossible.* I didn't say anything out loud, but I'm pretty sure my face revealed everything going on inside my head. I have a terrible poker face.

Mr. Goodson shrugged his shoulders and went back in his classroom (probably to crush more candy), leaving me and Mr. Clarence in the hallway. The final bell rang, so Mr. Clarence walked me to class so the teacher wouldn't mark me tardy.

"Listen, Plum, I know that seems like a lot and you're kind of overwhelmed right now," he said. "But hear me out. I think you can do it. I saw that you have a new friend. Ollie, right?"

"I have two friends now," I muttered.

"Two? That's great! Maybe the three of you could divide and conquer. This might be good for you. It will force you to take on a project that you care about, and it will force you to get out there and meet some of your fellow students. I know you think they're all jerks, but the bulk of the students here are good kids."

I mumbled something like, "I'll think about it."

155

And then he said, "Great," and handed me a piece of paper with 250 blank lines.

Plum's Punch List:

1. Cleaning someone else's house while on vacation
2. Bees
3. Anyone whose job is to embroider "This EpiPen Belongs to Plum" on a quilted pouch
4. People who say "easy peasy" about something that's actually really hard
5. 250 blank lines

Thursday
September 8

Quelle surprise. Pax said he'd help me with my petition. Honestly, I was a little stunned. No, I was super stunned. I think the bee stings affected his brain or something. Either that or my buzz cut was getting me some major sympathy points.

He passed the petition around his homeroom and got fourteen signatures just like that. Shocker, they were all girls who fell for his big bright puppy-dog eyes. I asked something like thirty people to sign the petition. A third of them said "No," a third of them pretended like they couldn't hear me and/or understand me, and the other third asked me for ID to prove I was an actual SPHS student (and after I showed it to them, they still refused to sign). It is not going well.

Mr. Clarence emailed Mom and told her about the French Club petition. Guess who was ALL OVER IT? She thought we should make posters and stuff to hang in the hallways encouraging kids to sign up. I thought that was a waste of poster board. Ollie thought we should use social media. Start a Snapchat campaign or something. That sounded like a waste of Wi-Fi. None of the kids from SPHS follow me on social media, so it would be like yelling into a black hole. Fadia thought we should offer a giveaway. Anyone who signed the petition would be automatically entered into a drawing for a new iPhone.

"Who's going to buy the iPhone to give away?" I asked.

"That's the beauty of it," Fadia said. "We just never draw. If we're asked, we say we drew and some rando sophomore no one's ever heard of won."

"What if a teacher asks for the name?" Ollie said.

"We make one up. We'll say his name is Ben Dover," Fadia said. "Or Amanda Hump."

"First of all," Mom said, "that's disgusting—and hilarious—but mostly disgusting. Second of all, that's illegal, Fadia. You can't run a contest and then not give away the prize."

"I agree," Ollie said. "Let's stick with posters and social media."

I could see Fadia was bummed, but her idea was out there, y'know? Besides, Mr. Clarence has been working with high school students for twenty-five years; he would be on to "Ben Dover" in about two seconds.

"Knock yourselves out," I told Mom and Ollie. I'd let them both do whatever they wanted. As long as I didn't have to talk to any more people and try to get signatures, I was good.

By morning I had eight posters Mom made. Her Cricut machine was literally smoking, and she was completely out of glue sticks and glitter. You'd never guess that my mom was a crafter. She keeps this obsession of hers on the down-low. She scoffs at the moms who spend their days repurposing soup cans into pencil holders or wreaths for the front door, but it's only because she sucks at crafting. She has spent hundreds of dollars on rubber stamps and ribbon that she's ruined trying to recreate things she saw on Pinterest. Even though she sucks at crafting, it doesn't stop her from trying. The letters on the posters were a bit wonky and she didn't do a very good job budgeting her glitter. It was clear she didn't plan ahead, so only half the letters on the eighth poster were glittered. But everything was spelled right and I didn't have to lift a finger, so I didn't complain.

I was shocked to see that the posters actually worked. I managed to get a few hung up in the ninth-grade pod before school started and by lunch I had people seeking me out to sign my petition. I left Ollie and Fadia in the cafeteria to collect more signatures while I ducked out to hang up posters in the tenth-grade pod. I taped the petition to the front of my locker so people could sign during passing periods and by the end of the day I had over 100 signatures. Between Mom's posters and Pax's puppy-dog eyes, I was almost halfway to my goal and I still hadn't hit the upperclassmen yet.

After the last bell, Fadia and I went to the eleventh-grade pod to hang up some of Mom's posters. I felt like a golden goddess. That's where Emberleigh and her goon squad found me.

"What is she even doing here?" Fadia whispered to me.

I shrugged. I was beginning to think Emberleigh just follows me around.

"Girl needs a life," Fadia whispered.

Emberleigh got out her phone and started snapping pictures of my posters. "What are you doing?" I asked her.

"I'm sending these to my mother," she said.

"Why?"

Emberleigh stopped what she was doing and turned to me, her eyes narrowing. "Did you make these posters yourself?"

Her question caught me by surprise. *Why did she ask me that?* I wondered. "No," I said carefully. "My mom made them."

A huge, cold smile spread across her face. One time at the zoo I saw a snake eat a frightened mouse. Emberleigh looked just like that snake right before it devoured the mouse. "I knew it!" she crowed. "*That's* why I'm sending pictures to my mother."

I still didn't get it. I looked at Fadia, who appeared to be just as confused as me. "So what if she made the posters?" Fadia asked.

Emberleigh shook her head with mock sadness. "It's a shame that you didn't read the school handbook before you started this little venture of yours, Plum," she said. "If you had, then you'd know that all school petitions must be orchestrated and promoted *entirely* by SPHS students. No teachers or parents may help in *any* way. Imagine if someone's mother was a professional artist and she made all the posters for her child? That student would have an unfair advantage over everyone else."

I felt sick to my stomach. Was she telling the truth? "But my mom isn't a professional artist," I croaked.

Savannah piped up, "Your mother is a professional writer. Her words are more compelling than others'."

The four of them nodded in unison.

I looked at my posters.

Parlez-vous Français? Non?
Want to learn?
Sign the petition on locker 378
and help us bring a French teacher to SPHS!
Merci beaucoup!

Yes, my mother is a professional writer, but come on, that was not her best work. Not even close, amiright?

"I'm texting my mother now. The signatures you've collected for your petition are completely null and void, Plum," sneered Emberleigh.

Glynis cackled evilly and tore down my poster and stomped on it.

"Whoa, Glynis," cautioned Kalista. "That was a tad harsh."

"Who knew you had a heart under all that ice, Kalista?" Fadia said.

Kalista glared at her.

"Shut up, Fatty-uh," Savannah said.

Fadia smirked. "I'm not even fat, you know that, right?"

"Whatever," Savannah said. "Just shut up. You're not even a part of this."

"Yeah," said Glynis. "When did you join the Pink Ladies, Fadia? I thought you were smarter than that."

Savannah laughed. "Plum's not even a Pink Lady anymore. With that hairdo she looks like some boy-band reject."

"Totally," Glynis said.

"Enough!" Emberleigh said, she put her phone in her pocket. "It's done. My mother is *all over* this. Let's go."

I waited for them to disappear in a cloud of black smoke, but instead they sauntered down the hall like they owned the place.

"Ignore them," Fadia said. "They can't do anything to you."

Fadia was wrong.

Mr. Clarence called Mom on her cell phone before we even got home.

"I'm in the car," Mom said. "Plum's with me and you're on speakerphone."

Mr. Clarence explained that while Mom's posters were absolutely wonderful, unfortunately they were a violation of SPHS policy. Mom was furious. She said, "I'm trying to help my kid here, Mr. Clarence. I can't help it that your school is so backassward that we must actually petition to get a French teacher! *That* is the real problem here, Mr. Clarence. You understand that, right? It's as if culture means nothing to this school district."

Mr. Clarence sucked in a lot of air, but he didn't say anything. He couldn't argue. It *was* ridiculous only one foreign language was offered, and I think he knew that.

Mom kept arguing. "Plus, I would think that as an administrator, you'd be happy to have some parent involvement! Plum shouldn't be jeopardized because she has parents who want to help her achieve her goals! There are thousands—no, millions—of children out there who have parents who don't give a hoot about them. Normally schools want parents who are plugged in and want to help."

"*Too much* parent involvement is actually a bigger problem at our school," Mr. Clarence muttered.

"Well, I can't help it that they're all snowflakes, Mr. Clarence," Mom said. "Especially that Emberleigh. She's done nothing but make Plum's life miserable since school started. That girl has everyone at SPHS snowed."

"She's a hose-beast," I chimed in.

"Plum!" Mom scolded me.

"I realize that Plum and Emberleigh have gotten off on the wrong foot, and I'm actually working on a way to encourage them to mend their rift and work together."

"Work together" did not sound like a very good idea. "That's a hard pass," I said.

Mom shook her head. "What do you propose, Mr. Clarence?"

"Well, Emberleigh is right. The names Plum has collected aren't allowed because of the interference from you, Mrs. Parrish. You'll need to start again, Plum, and this time it will need to be completely student-driven."

I groaned loudly.

"I'm aware that you don't know a lot of students at SPHS," Mr. Clarence continued, "but Emberleigh does. I would like to propose that you two work together and collect the signatures as a team. Emberleigh and her friends have the connections and you have the passion, Plum. It would be a perfect partnership."

I just sat there, completely dumbfounded. If I'd been the one driving I would have driven us off the road and into a ditch at that moment. If I'd been sitting across the table from Mr. Clarence right then, I would have reached over and slapped him across his dull-witted face.

Stupid me. I really thought Mr. Clarence was different. I thought he understood me. Clearly I was wrong. Utterly and totally wrong. Mr. Clarence wasn't any different than Mr. Cutler. They all think Emberleigh is the Queen Bee of the school. They think that sure, she has a little sting, but it's a small price to pay to be in the presence of such greatness. Ugh.

"No can do, Mr. Clarence," I said, all weird and cocky.

Mom whipped her head toward me and cocked an eyebrow, *Are you sure?* Yup. I wasn't going to budge.

"Excuse me?" Mr. Clarence said.

I was ready to give up. The whole French Club thing had become a nightmare. I had no idea it would be such a disaster when I agreed to it. I loved Madame O'Malley and I loved being a part of French Club at my old school, but it was becoming way too much angst for me. I didn't need friends that badly. Ollie and Fadia were enough. I had a nice spot in the girls' bathroom where I could eat lunch on the days they were absent. I was going to be fine.

FINE, I TELL YA! FINE!

Besides, high school was only four more years. In a few years I'll go to college where it's going to be sooooo much better.

In the meantime, if I changed my mind and wanted a French Club at SPHS, I'd do it on my own. I might not know a lot of people, but I'm not a social moron. I CAN talk to people. I CAN start over. I didn't need Emberleigh. I didn't need to bow down and kiss her (probably fake) UGG boots.

"I can't pair up with the Queen Bee and her *wannabees*. I'm pretty sure I'm allergic to bees. Right, Mom?" I said.

Mom frowned, but then smiled at me. She mouthed, "Are you sure?" and when I nodded she said, "Right! Plum will figure this out on her own—without any interference from me or her dad. Goodbye, Mr. Clarence."

And then Mom hung up on him. LIKE A BOSS!

Plum's Punch List:

1. The SPHS handbook that no one thought to read
2. Overbearing mothers who get their noses in my business and thereby ruin everything
3. Petitions
4. Mr. Clarence

Friday

September 9

We decided to try again, but we'd do it our way, so tonight we made new posters. It took us hours, but they look spectacular. Who knew Fadia was a mad genius with a glue gun and glitter? She should have mentioned it in between her Ponzi schemes and fake giveaway ideas. Ollie did an excellent job supervising and making sure Fadia had good music to keep her motivated, and I kept us all fed and hydrated—priorities, I have them. Mom did not lift a finger to help us. I asked her to help me by putting ice in the water glasses and she pretended to faint and yelled, "What if someone sees me doing that? I don't want my actions misconstrued! Pretend like I'm not here!" She wouldn't even offer a word of advice and/or encouragement lest she be accused of over-involvement, but she was totally taking notes, because Fadia's results were about 1,000 times better than hers.

We'd finished our work and the three of us were hanging out in my room.

"Mr. Clarence is a spoon!" I said.

"Umm, a what?" Ollie asked.

"A spoon," I said. "My mom says it all the time. It means that you're too stupid to be trusted with a knife and fork, so you can only have a spoon."

"That is completely random but kind of genius," said Fadia.

"It's not one of her best insults, but it works well for this situation."

"I still don't get it. Why is he a spoon?" Ollie said.

"Because he's too dumb to see that Emberleigh is full of crap. They all are! He and Cutler and all the rest of the teachers. They all think she's so perfect and they let her get away with murder!"

"That's just life, Plum," Fadia said. "Look around. All the beautiful people are the ones who never have to follow the rules. We're the suckers who do all the work and then get stepped on."

"Follow the rules?" Ollie scoffed. "Bish, please. They *make* the rules. And they're constantly changing the rules. We make it two steps forward and then we're pushed one step back. Look at this petition nonsense. We've been working nonstop on this thing. We were *this close* to getting it done and then Emberleigh and Clarence and Cutler—all of them—they moved the finish line."

"Exactly!" I said. "So why are we even doing this?"

Ollie looked shocked. "I thought it was what you wanted. You said you wanted to keep going."

"I had nothing better going on," said Fadia.

I sighed heavily. "I'm so confused," I admitted. "We've put a crap ton of effort into this and I don't really want it to all go to waste, but what are we doing, you guys? What's the point? I'm sure they'll figure out a way to throw up another roadblock."

"You can't flake out on us now," Fadia said. "I know I act like I don't care either way, but I do care. I want you to win, Plum. I could give a rat's ass about French. I signed the petition, but I probably won't even sign up. I like Spanish. But I want to see some change around here. I want to see someone actually get something done. That's why I'm here. Also, the food's good."

"Do you think I'm flaking out?" I asked Ollie.

He was sheepish. "Well, you are hard to read. I mean, at first you were like, 'Never again!' And then you were like, 'I've got nachos, let's make posters.' And now you're like, 'I give up.' Wah. It's kind of exhausting."

"Well, I'm exhausted!" I whined. "And I'm confused. I'm pissed I even have to do this. They should just have French. What's wrong with this school!?"

Fadia shrugged. "Well, at this point, the posters are done. We've done the hard part. We got almost 250 signatures in one day, we can do it again."

I nodded. "You're right. But we're not going to sweat it this time. We'll put up the new posters that we made and we'll get the signatures. If we don't have enough by the end of next week, screw this, we're out. Life's too short. I'll join Spanish and keep quiet."

"Really?" asked Ollie. "You'd just walk away from French Club? Just like that?"

I nodded.

"What if we get enough signatures?" Fadia asked.

I shrugged. "Well, then I guess we move forward with the meeting at the district offices and see how that goes. But what I'm trying to say is I'm sick of wasting so much time and energy on this. I loved Madame O'Malley and French Club back in Jersey, but the one here could totally suck balls and then what?"

"Mmm, balls," Ollie said, grinning.

"Ewww!" Fadia laughed and threw a pillow at him.

"Ollie!" I threw a stuffed animal at him.

We all collapsed into a fit of laughter.

And for just a split second I was happy. Really, truly happy. I haven't felt that way in months, not since Mom and Dad had announced our move. I felt warm and giddy inside. I felt understood, and I felt like Ollie and Fadia *got* me. If the petition succeeds, great. But if it doesn't, who cares? I don't need a French Club as long as I have them.

Plum's Punch List:

1. None—I found my tribe.

Saturday
September 10

I found out that Fadia, Ollie, and I aren't the only ones with a petition.

Mrs. Davidson, Emberleigh's mother, has been hard at work too. She got over 1,000 people to sign a petition to ban Mom's books from the county library. What is the deal with this town and freaking petitions? I swear, I'd barely even heard the word before we moved here, let alone signed one. Ugh. I was up in my room when the notice arrived. The library sent Mom this super formal letter—the mailman had to come to the door and get Mom's signature for it and everything. When Mom read the letter she screamed.

She screamed so loud I could hear her through my noise-canceling headphones. That's pretty freaking loud. I went tearing downstairs because I thought maybe she'd found Dad's lifeless body on the couch or something. I have this irrational fear my parents will die in their sleep and leave me and Pax to fend for ourselves. I realize it's not a normal fear, but surely by now you know I'm not normal, right? Instead, I found her in the front hall rereading the letter.

"What's going on, Mom?"

Mom read aloud, "Dear Lacy Drawers, There has been a formal complaint lodged against you and your work. It has been deemed inappropriate for the general public. It has been called unseemly, pornographic, and obscene. After reviewing the complaint and determining it had the necessary signatures, we scrutinized your complete works and found that they do not meet our decency guidelines, thus, we have no choice but to pull all copies from the shelves of our twelve locations and make a notation that we will not stock any future works."

"Who did this to you?" I asked.

She chortled. "Do you have to ask? When someone tells you who they are, believe them, Plum. I am positive our good friend Mrs. Davidson is behind this."

"Emberleigh's mom?"

Poor Mom. Can you believe it? How could Mrs. Davidson do this to her? Why does she hate us so much? I felt so bad for Mom. I couldn't imagine someone going to so much work to silence me. It's like Mrs. Davidson has absolutely no life. Who has time for this kind of crap? She desperately needs a job or a hobby or something!

I was working out a plan to slash the tires on Mrs. Davidson's SUV or shave her stupid dog when I realized Mom was laughing. "Why are you laughing, Mom? Have you gone loony? Is this the final straw and your brain has finally snapped?"

"Because I'm happy, Plum. So very happy." Mom smiled broadly.

"Happy? Umm … what?"

"Ben!" Mom yelled. "Great news! I've been banned!"

Dad was in the living room and he whooped and threw his newspaper in the air. "It's about time!"

I was so confused. Apparently it's a *good* thing to have a banned book? "This is good news?" I asked.

"Yes! Now my work is *infamous*," Mom cheered.

"Hopefully this will catch on," said Dad, clapping his hands. "A few more library systems and bada bing bada boom, you'll be a superstar." He did lame-o jazz hands.

"If it does, I'm going to send that chick a bouquet of flowers," Mom said.

"It's the least you could do," agreed Dad. "Better yet, send her a bouquet of banned books."

I was utterly confused. I was like, what is happening? Why isn't Mom pissed? Why isn't she mortified? I would die—literally—if someone went to all that trouble to let our whole county know I sucked. I mean, wouldn't we all? Why was Mom acting like it was awesome?

Pax came into the kitchen to grab some food. "What's all the hubbub?" he asked.

"Emberleigh's mother got Mom's books banned from the county library," I said.

"Nice!" Pax said, giving Mom a high five.

"Am I in the fricking *Twilight Zone?*" I asked.

Mom immediately got on the phone and started calling all the local news stations to let them know just how unfairly she'd been treated because: censorship, bad, First Amendment, good, blah, blah.

A camera crew showed up at our door before lunch. Mom acted all surprised they were there, but she had on a full face of makeup and her hair was on point. *Puhleeze.* I was so on to her.

They sat in our living room where some insanely bouncy blond woman— Merry Joy? I couldn't remember her idiotic obviously made-up newscaster name—tried to nod sympathetically while Mom worked up an actual tear. "This is my livelihood, you understand," Mom said, her voice getting all croaky. "I have children to support. I'm being vilified here for no reason other than Mrs. Davidson doesn't care for my genre. No one held a gun to her head and forced her to read it. I'm bringing entertainment to millions of people across the world, and now our county will be denied that pleasure."

I was sort of lurking in the doorway watching from behind the camera when the bouncy blond—Hope Alive?—saw me. "Would you join us, Plum?" she asked. And when I stood there stupidly not reacting or replying, she turned to Mom. "Her name *is* Plum, right?"

Mom nodded and dabbed the corner of her eye. "Yes. Plum, Constant Grace is speaking to you," Mom said.

Constant Grace! That was it, I thought.

I told you her name was idiotic. It was like she showed up for her first job as a newscaster and when her boss heard her name was Mary Smith he was like, "Oh no! That simply won't do! Your new name is," he flipped through a dictionary on his desk and stopped on a random page, "Constant," flip, flip, flip, "Grace! Constant Grace reporting live from the scene of the crime. Constant Grace has the scoop on the scandal at city hall."

Constant Grace tried again. "Plum, please sit down with your mom and give her a hug, would ya?"

My feet stayed firmly planted. Mom might have known the news crew was coming, but I sure didn't. I wasn't dressed for a television interview. I was wearing ratty sweatpants and one of Dad's old T-shirts. My black eyeliner was smudged under my eyes and down my cheek and my hair has never grown so fast in my life. Even though it's only two inches long, it can get really fluffy. And my roots are already demanding a touch-up, but I'm afraid to ask Mom to take me to get it done, because that is not a battle I'm prepared to wage yet. I looked like a cross between a raccoon and a porcupine. There was no way in hell I was going to get in front of that camera.

Mom waved me over. "Come sit by me, Plummy." She patted the sofa cushion next to her.

"I-I-I'd rather not," I stammered, hoping Mom would see I wasn't fit to be on television. "I haven't showered…I'm not dressed…I'm not…uh." The cameraman was a man and I didn't know how to tell Mom I wasn't wearing a bra without embarrassing the crap out of myself! I didn't have plans to leave the house, so I was freeboobing it.

"That's okay! I don't mind," Constant Grace said. "It will actually make your mom seem more human. She's got a tough audience to please, and it might help for them to see that her daughter isn't perfect."

I was all, *Umm…thanks, I guess?* I mean, come on, what kind of backhanded compliment was that? So rude!! I glared at Constant Grace, but I kept my opinions to myself.

Constant Grace shrugged and sighed theatrically. "Well, if you're not interested in helping your mom, that's fine too." She reached over and patted Mom's hand sadly.

OH KALE NO SHE DIDN'T! Yeah, she did!

She totally called me out. She made me look disloyal. Like I don't love Mom! What was I supposed to do then? Mom was looking at me with sad eyes and the cameraman looked at me like I was the worst example of a daughter he'd ever seen. There was nothing I could do except cuss out Constant Grace in my head. I huffed and puffed, but I finally shuffled over to the sofa and plopped down beside Mom.

"You're going to want to sit up straight, Plum," Mom whispered in my ear, tugging on my arm.

"Why?" I grumbled. "I can't look any worse than I do now."

Famous last words. I was so, so, so, so, so, so, so wrong! You know that saying about the camera adding ten pounds? Yeah, that's when you're sitting up straight, sucking in your tummy and angling your chin just right. When you're slumped on an overstuffed couch in shapeless clothes, no bra, and no makeup, you look about 100 pounds heavier. But I didn't know that at the time. It wasn't until many hours later when the segment ran on the nightly news and I saw what I at first assumed was a giant pile of dirty laundry with a double chin and eyes on the couch next to Mom that I realized why I should have heeded her warning.

Unfortunately in addition to ignoring Mom's sage advice, I let Constant Grace ask me a barrage of questions I was woefully unprepared for.

Questions like, "Have you ever read any of your mother's books?"

I answered, "No, I'm not allowed."

Constant Grace's crazy dark eyebrows shot up. "Oh reeeeeeeally," she said. "Why is that exactly?"

"They're inappropriate," I said.

"For *children*," Mom interjected, nudging my leg.

"Yes, for children," I parroted.

"Are you a child still, Plum?"

"Umm … kinda?"

"So you only read children's books?"

"No! Of course not!"

"Ah, interesting. So you've probably read some adult books by now, haven't you? Why not your mother's?"

"Uhh … I'm not a fan."

"Of your mother's work?" Constant Grace asked. Mom sucked in her breath.

"God, no!" I exclaimed, all panicky. "I'm not a fan of her genre! I don't read romance."

"What do you think of your mother's job?"

"It's fine, I guess."

"You *guess*? Do you wish she had a normal job like a normal mother?"

"I don't know. Maybe. I don't know what normal moms do."

"They don't write racy books, that's for sure," Constant Grace said, all triumphant. Her eyes went cold and dead and she pursed her lips.

Oh, crap! You see, all that time Mom thought Constant Grace was on her side, but she wasn't. No one was. Constant Grace was on Mrs. Davidson's side. She *wanted* Mom's books to be banned. I had to say something to help Mom. I couldn't just sit there and not defend her. Mom needed me! So I said, "If being a normal mom means you act like the moms around here, then no, I don't want a normal mom," I said.

"Plum!" Mom chuckled nervously and patted my hand.

I shook her off and kept going, "I don't want a mom who wears tennis skirts all day and drinks green smoothies instead of eating solid food. I don't want a mom who spends her days writing passive-aggressive notes on the neighborhood message boards about someone's grass that's a centimeter too long. I don't want a mom who lives vicariously through her children and has no life of her own. I don't want a mom whose entire existence is to drive her kids from one over-scheduled event to another. My mom is awesome. She is funny and she's creative and she takes good care of me and Pax. She taught us how to read and how to draw. She helps us with our homework, she loves us, *and* she writes saucy books!"

Mom smiled and her eyes were shiny. All I could think was, *God, please don't cry, Mom. Blubbering is the last thing we need right now.*

"Whoa, Plum! That's a lot of anger you have there," Constant Grace said, frowning.

"Plum's not angry," Mom said, throwing an arm around my shoulder. "She's passionate. She is a true and loyal person who loves fiercely and protects those that she loves. You wish you had someone as wonderful as Plum in your corner!"

Constant Grace help up her hands. "If you say so, Lacy." She turned to me, her fake innocent eyes all wide. "Is that what you're doing, Plum? Are you trying to protect your mother from Mrs. Davidson?"

I shrugged. At that point I was so irritated. It was clear Constant Grace wanted me to say something bad about Mom, but there was no way I was going to do that. This was all Mrs. Davidson's fault. She started it! It couldn't go any worse at that point. I mean, come on, I looked terrible and Constant Grace kept trying to bait me, so I just said what was on mind. "Mrs. Davidson has had it out for my mom since we first met her. She was, like, so mean to her. She's a bully. I thought bullies didn't exist once you were an adult, but I guess I was wrong. She pushes people around, and now she's trying to push my mom around. She and her horrible daughter, Emberleigh! Emberleigh got my French Club petition banned too, you know. They have nothing better to do than to make our lives miserable. It's like those two are obsessed with us or something."

"Obsessed?" Constant Grace smiled coldly at me.

"Yeah, they're obsessed with us. Totally!"

"Do you agree with Plum?" Constant Grace asked Mom.

"'Obsessed' is a strong word," Mom said carefully. "I will say I've never encountered someone quite like Mrs. Davidson. She has the drive and determination to ruin my livelihood unlike anyone I've ever seen. She definitely needs a job or something because she has entirely too much time on her hands, and for some reason tormenting our family has become her pet project. I don't know why. We're neighbors. Our children are classmates. And yet, she's relentless in her pursuit to put me out of a job and bring misery to our family. It's gone beyond morals or personal taste in literature; she has made it personal."

"So you do think Mrs. Davidson is attacking you personally? What makes you so important that she'd only go after you?" Constant Grace asked.

Mom looked stunned. "Oh, I didn't mean to imply that I'm anything special. I'm not saying that I'm the only author battling people like Mrs. Davidson. My whole industry and genre are being attacked daily, but I'm not the only author out there suffering from censorship. Please, don't make this all about me. Many of us are victims of ignorant individuals who are acting out to enforce their own values on the rest of the population. If Mrs. Davidson doesn't want to read my books, then she shouldn't, but her personal beliefs shouldn't overshadow others' rights. Reading books that make us uncomfortable makes us better people."

Constant Grace must not have known what to say to Mom after that, because she just turned to the camera and said, "There certainly is a lot to think on with this debate. Weigh in on Twitter and let us know what *you* think!"

She held her smile and her rigorous posture for another thirty seconds or so and then the cameraman put down his camera and said, "Looked great, Constant."

Constant Grace flipped her hair over her shoulder and smiled her toothiest smile at me and Mom and said, "Be sure to watch yourselves tonight on the five o'clock news."

"Thanks for doing this, Constant," Mom said, extending her hand.

Constant Grace put her limp hand into Mom's. "Happy to bring a light to this important subject."

After she left, Mom said Constant Grace's hand felt like a cold fish. Big surprise there.

Plum's Punch List:

1. Constant Grace

Monday

September 20

DISASTER.

Such a bloody disaster. If I wasn't already an outcast at school, I am certainly one now.

The Constant Grace interview ran last night on the five o'clock news. And the six o'clock. And the eight o'clock. And the ten o'clock. And then again this morning. Who knew the news was on so many times during the day? Wasn't there a *Seinfeld* rerun they could air or something? When did the news become so popular?

The interview was horrible. Constant Grace (or someone) edited Mom a lot and made her sound a little bit whiny, sort of entitled, and hella preachy. Mom was horrified at first until her agent called and said she was seeing a real upswing in sales. Books that hadn't sold a copy in ten years were flying off the shelves—well, into people's online carts—in droves. Bookstores and libraries in other cities were buying copies to feature on their "banned books" displays. Her agent called it nothing short of a miracle. At that point Mom popped open a bottle of champagne and toasted Constant Grace and her team.

"Any publicity is good publicity," Dad said, toasting her.

Because Mom wasn't upset, I was feeling pretty good about the interview when I got to school. Sure, I had looked like a pile of laundry with a double chin and eyes, but Mom had looked great and even though the interview was skewed weirdly, it still got her the results she was hoping for. In fact, her success inspired me to get back to my petition and to really hit it hard today.

I found Ollie right away and told him today was the day to blow out the numbers and finish the damn thing. He agreed and to pump us up we did this really elaborate high-five/chest-bump thing I've seen Pax and his bros do. That's when the Queen Bee and her Wannabees came around the corner. Emberleigh narrowed her eyes as soon as she saw me.

That's when I knew it was on like Donkey Kong.

"You," Emberleigh sneered, stopping in her tracks.

I shrugged. "Me," I said. Ollie snickered a little and nudged me, giving me a bit of his confidence.

"What is wrong with you?" Emberleigh demanded.

I didn't think she was looking for a real answer, so I decided to go with snarky. "There's nothing wrong with me," I said. "I'm perfect with a capital P."

"No," Emberleigh said. "You're insane with a capital I."

"I can't even believe that you went on television and told everyone that Emberleigh and her mother are *obsessed* with you," Savannah said.

"As if," Kalista said.

"You wish," Glynis said.

"You are so weird," Emberleigh said.

At this point everyone who had been milling around the lockers waiting for the bell to ring suddenly took a great interest in what was going down in our row of lockers. I saw Fadia peek around the corner with her phone pointed at us.

"My mom says your mom is jealous of Mrs. Davidson," said Alice, the girl with the locker next to mine (you know, the one I've never spoken to).

"My dad said that the interview was a pathetic grab for attention," her scrawny boyfriend, Kyle, said.

Emberleigh sneered at me. I wanted to smack the smug look off her face. She was like a boil on my butt. I hated her.

Another girl came over and said, "Wait. I'm so confused. What did I miss? What are you guys all talking about?"

Her friend next to her filled her in…sorta. "So, Plum's mom is some kind of freaky writer woman who writes completely inappropriate books—"

"Well…" I tried to interrupt her, but she held up a hand to silence me.

"You said it yourself, Plum. Anyway, her mom is writing this trash—"

"It's not trash!" Ollie said.

"How would you know?" Savannah asked.

Ollie turned red. "I just do," he stammered.

"Oh my God! Have you read Mrs. Parrish's books?" Emberleigh cackled.

Ollie looked sick for a moment, but then he regained his composure. "I certainly have," he said, bursting with confidence. "And I'm a proud card-carrying member of her fan club."

Yeah, Ollie has joined Lacy's Lovelies. I was shocked, but I couldn't even think about that, because suddenly questions were coming from all over the place and I had no idea who was asking what.

"If it's not trash, then why doesn't she put her real name on the covers of her books?"

"What? Her name isn't on the covers?"

"No," Emberleigh said. "She's too embarrassed to put her name on the covers. So she uses a fake name."

Alice turned on me. "Is that true?"

"Umm…well…" I tried to think of what to say. *Why did Mom use a fake name?* I wondered. *Maybe she* was *embarrassed.*

"She uses a fake name to protect her identity, you twit," Ollie said. "Duh. She's a BFD and she doesn't want her superfan stalkers showing up at her house or following her around the grocery store or whatever."

"Well, she must not be too worried about her privacy since she went on TV last night and put all of her business out there," Kyle said.

"You wouldn't even begin to understand Mrs. P's reasoning. You're so out of her league," Ollie sniffed.

"All I know is I would die. Literally die if my mom wrote smut and accused people of fake obsessions," Glynis said.

"Yeah, why can't your mom just be normal like everyone else's?" Emberleigh asked.

I was like, *There's that word again. Why's everyone saying Mom isn't normal? What is so abnormal about her?*

"My mother *is* normal!" I yelled, fighting back tears. I lost it at that point. *She is normal! She is! She is! She is!* My brain screamed. I was reeling and then I finally let the doubt creep in. *Isn't she? God, why can't Mom be a part-time receptionist at a doctor's office? Why does she have to cuss like a sailor and write books that people probably whack off to?* I am not proud of feeling this way. I'm just glad I didn't say it out loud.

Ollie put an arm around me and glared at Emberleigh. "Why are you such a harpy, Emberleigh?" he asked. "Do you get off on making everyone around you feel like shit all the time?"

"Stay out of it, Ollie," said Savannah. "This isn't even about you!"

"*You* stay out of it, Savannah," Ollie screeched. "Why do you always rush in to fight Emberleigh's fights?"

"No one is fighting my fights, Ollie," Emberleigh said. "God, you're so gay!"

Savannah got right up next to Ollie's ear and whispered, "That's right. You're a *faggot.*"

Glynis squealed. "Look at you, Plum. You're such a loser. You hang out with a faggot and Jihad Jane. Those are the only friends you can find. Even your own twin brother won't hang out with you."

Up until that point I'd been sort of half-sobbing on Ollie and trying to figure out a way to salvage what little reputation I had left, but I snapped out of it when I heard Savannah and Glynis. I felt Ollie tense up and I waited for him to go full nuclear on those two jackwagons. But he didn't. Instead, he sort of sagged against me. I couldn't believe it. Ollie was the stronger one of the two of us. If he couldn't take any more, how could I? I looked to Fadia. She was still lurking and she had visible tears in her eyes. I felt deflated.

I looked at Emberleigh, Savannah, and Glynis all huddled together, whispering and sneering at us. Everyone else just stood around awkwardly trying to pretend like the insides of their lockers were so fascinating and they didn't hear Savannah's or Glynis's vile remarks. I knew many were horrified, but they were chickenshits. Except for Kalista, maybe? She stood apart from her pack. She looked like she couldn't decide if she should join them or run away. I made eye contact with her and her eyes were so sad. So tired. She was exhausted too.

I turned on Emberleigh. "I hate you," I said, struggling to keep my voice calm. "You are a horrible person who imposes your will on those around you because you hate yourself. You only feel good when you're putting others down. You keep Savannah and Glynis and Kalista on short leashes and you belittle them so that they'll never feel confident enough to take your spot. I'm looking around this school, Emberleigh, and I can see that you have sucked the life out of all of us." I spread my arms wide. "I'm sick of it and I think they are too! I am sick of being made to feel less than. I am sick of watching the teachers and staff in the school practically bow down every time you walk in a room. I am tired of your meddling mother attacking my mom. I've had enough! You don't get to fill your reserves by calling me and my friends names. You don't get to step on us so you can climb higher. This stops now. I don't care who you are, I don't care who your mother is. I don't care how many boots you lick and how many asses you kiss. I see right through you. I see your black heart and your vile soul. I refuse to let you hold any power over me. I am stronger than you. I am better than you. Now, get out of my face!"

Emberleigh's mouth flapped open and closed, but no sound emerged.

"I've had enough, too, Emberleigh," Kalista said, stepping between us.

"You?" Emberleigh said, her face contorting into fury. "I *made* you, Kalista. I plucked you out of obscurity. You were nothing until I decided you were something and now you're going to turn on me and join this…band of losers?"

"We're not losers," I said. "We're just normal people who you deemed unworthy and uncool."

"Well, Kalista, I hope you enjoyed your time with me, because I will never speak to you again. Oh, and by the way, I'll be sure to let everyone know that your mom is a pill popper."

Kalista moved faster than I ever imagined she could. "ARGH!!!" she screamed as she lunged for Emberleigh.

I don't remember much after that. It was a total blur. I know they tussled.

They rolled around on the floor a lot. There was a lot of screaming and hair-pulling—more Kalista than Emberleigh since Emberleigh spent most of her energy crying, "Help me, Savannah!" But Savannah didn't intervene. She didn't join in, but she didn't stop the fight either. I don't know how long they fought, but I do I know that it was Mr. Clarence and Mr. Goodson who broke them up.

Mr. Clarence grabbed Kalista and me. "Hey," I protested. "I didn't do anything! It wasn't me this time."

"Yeah, we'll see about that," Mr. Clarence said.

Mr. Goodson sent Emberleigh to the nurse's office to treat her "injuries."

"Please. As if. She's such a faker," Ollie said.

"What's wrong with her?" I asked Mr. Clarence.

"She broke a…fingernail," he replied.

"Too bad. I was hoping it was her nose," said Kalista. "Her father paid a fortune for it over the summer."

His mustache wiggled, but just ever so slightly. He was definitely fighting a smile. If I had blinked, I would have missed it. "Let's go, you two."

"Where are you taking Plum?" Ollie asked. "She shouldn't be in trouble. This was Kalista's fight. Even Kalista shouldn't be in trouble. Emberleigh's had it coming for weeks."

"You come too, Mr. Bridgewater," Mr. Clarence said. "I want to speak to all of you." He sent Savannah and Glynis with Mr. Goodson.

Mr. Clarence took us to his office and I slumped down in the chair across from his desk. I waited for him to call Mom, but he didn't. He just sat there and stared at me and Ollie and Kalista.

Ollie got kind of fidgety, Kalista looked at her shoes, but I just stared Mr. Clarence down. Finally he spoke. "You want to tell me what I just witnessed?" he asked.

I shrugged. "A fight?"

"Your second one in," he consulted the calendar on his desk, "less than three weeks."

I shrugged again.

"I told you," Ollie said. "Plum wasn't fighting."

Kalista looked up. "It was me. I was the one who hit her. Plum only yelled at her."

"Plum didn't even touch Emberleigh," Ollie said. "This wasn't her fault."

"I suppose when she pushed Malcolm down the bleachers that wasn't her fault either?" Mr. Clarence said.

"Well, I-I," Ollie stammered. "I wasn't there for that incident, but I was there today and I can tell you that Plum was only *verbally* sparring. She was defending us—me and Fadia and everyone, really—from bullying."

"Bullying?" Mr. Clarence said, leaning forward in his chair. "That's a big word around here, Mr. Bridgewater. We take bullying very seriously here at Sunset Pines High School. We have zero tolerance for bullies."

"Well, good," Ollie said. "Then you should expel Emberleigh, Savannah, and Glynis."

"What did Emberleigh do, exactly?" Mr. Clarence looked directly at me. "Plum?"

I took a deep breath and thought. *Had Emberleigh bullied me? She had definitely made my life incredibly miserable and she'd said some hateful things to me, but was she a bully? Like, for real?* I wasn't sure. "Well, you know how she got me in trouble with my petition and stuff," I mumbled.

"I know that she brought it to our attention that you were in violation of the SPHS code of conduct."

"Her mom got my mom's book banned from the county library and the local bookstores and stuff."

"That doesn't sound like Emberleigh did anything against you in particular, Plum. That sounds like a beef between Mrs. Davidson and your mother. Anything else?"

"She never ate lunch with me!" I sobbed.

Mr. Clarence's brow furrowed. "What?"

"Mr. Cutler assigned her to be my peer model. She was supposed to show me around the school and eat lunch with me. She never ate lunch with me. She always dumped me. She made me feel stupid, and it was hard to ask anyone else to sit with me and so I ended up eating in the girls' bathroom." Hot tears burned my eyes. It might not be the true definition of bullying, but her actions were definitely hurtful.

"That's a hundred percent true," Kalista said. "Emberleigh put the word out that if anyone ate lunch with Plum they'd be exiled for, like, ever."

Mr. Clarence's face softened. "I see," he said, jotting a note down on the pad of paper in front of him. He turned to Ollie. "And what about you, Oliver? Do you have a formal complaint against Emberleigh?"

Ollie pursed his lips. "No," he admitted. "But I do have a complaint against Savannah and Glynis. They both said some demeaning and derogatory remarks about me and Fadia."

"What did they say?" Mr. Clarence asked.

"I refuse to say them out loud," Ollie said. "They were appalling." He got up and went to Mr. Clarence's side and whispered in his ear.

Mr. Clarence's face turned red with anger and he jotted more on the pad. "Now, *that* sounds like bullying!"

"They've said even worse in private," Kalista said. "Emberleigh's a cancer, Mr. Clarence. She infects everyone around her."

"What's going on with you, Kalista?" Mr. Clarence said. "I thought you were one of her closest friends."

"I was until today. Today was my breaking point. I was tired of being told who I can and can't be friends with, what to wear, what to say, what to *think*. And then the one time I stand up to her, she tells everyone my biggest secret. I confided in her about my mom's problem, like, as a friend. It was private! It's a sickness, y'know? My mom isn't well. She needs help, not to be ridiculed. I trusted Emberleigh and she betrayed me. That's why I hit her."

"I think I understand," Mr. Clarence said.

The door behind us opened and the nurse deposited Emberleigh in the room. "She really needs to go home, Mr. Clarence. She's faint and definitely shocked by this senseless attack on her," the nurse said. "I've already called her mother and she's on her way."

"That's fine," Mr. Clarence said. "Would you please take Kalista to your office and look her over?"

The nurse frowned, but said, "Of course. Come on, Kalista." Kalista went silently.

Mr. Clarence motioned to Emberleigh. "Have a seat, Emberleigh."

The only available seat was next to me. Emberleigh made this huge dramatic deal of dragging it far away from me so she'd be out of my reach.

Mr. Clarence waited until her theatrics were done and then he leaned way back in his chair and steepled his fingers. "I don't know what to do with you girls," he began. "I'm disappointed in the both of you. Emberleigh, you are supposedly one of the great leaders of this school. You are admired by your peers and your teachers. You are a born leader who can command people to do whatever you wish and to my dismay, time and time again I have witnessed you using this power for evil." I grinned when he said that. He turned his laser focus on me at that point. "And you, Plum Parrish. You are a new student in our school and I would think you would be doing whatever you could to find a way to join our community and get to know us, but instead you arrived with a chip on your shoulder and an ax to grind. You were never interested in becoming a real member of the SPHS family. You made it abundantly clear to anyone who came near you that you weren't interested in being their friend or joining their group."

I opened my mouth to argue, but I couldn't think what to say. Mr. Clarence had pretty much nailed it on the head. I hadn't even tried to join the Dorks or the Artsy Fartsies, I just assumed they wouldn't want me and so I rejected them before they could reject me. I had decided about 2.4 seconds after meeting Emberleigh that she was the worst and we'd never be friends. Yes, she'd been a headache since that moment, but maybe I had brought some of that on myself. I assumed that the cackling flap-mouthed hens that followed her around were also wastes of space and I had no intention of getting to know any of them. And then there was Malcolm. I was almost positive he was a loudmouth nitwit, but maybe I judged him too quickly and too harshly. I considered Malcolm again. Nah. I wasn't backing down on Malcolm. He was a dope who got what he deserved. Mr. Clarence was only partly right.

I was too busy contemplating my previous actions and I wasn't listening very closely to Mr. Clarence, so imagine my surprise when I heard him say, "… I should expel you both from school …"

"Expel us?" I said.

"Yes, all of you."

"But—" Ollie interjected.

Mr. Clarence held up a his hand. "But I won't. I am going to give you all one more chance, but there will be consequences."

"What kind of consequences?" Emberleigh huffed.

"You and your cohorts, including Kalista, will resign from the cheerleading squad."

"Are you insane?" Emberleigh screeched.

"It's either that or a week's suspension," Mr. Clarence said.

"I'll take the week. There is no way I'm quitting cheerleading. Savannah and Glynis will take the week, too."

"Let's let them make up their own minds for once, shall we?" Mr. Clarence said. I was grinning foolishly when he turned on me. "And you'll give up French Club."

"What?"

"I know that you think having French Club will fix all your problems, but it won't. If anything your attempt to form French Club has been an utter disaster. French Club was your thing at your old school. It's time to find your thing at your new school."

"But, Mr. Clarence," I said. "I've worked so hard and now you want me to just walk away?" Even though I'd already floated the idea of quitting, the hell I wanted it to be Mr. Clarence's doing. I wanted it to be my decision, not his!

"We'll take the week's suspension," Ollie said.

"Sorry, you two don't get a choice," Mr. Clarence said.

Plum's Punch List:

1. Emberleigh and her dumb-ass hive mind
2. Mr. Clarence and his bright ideas
3. French Club

Wednesday

September 21

Mom and Dad totally grounded me and I couldn't leave the house except to go to school. Everyone gave me plenty of space today. I am a pariah. Even Fadia kept her distance. I'm worried she isn't my friend anymore. I ate lunch with Ollie, but Fadia never showed up. When I asked where she was he said he had no idea; she hadn't returned his texts. I finally decided I couldn't take the uncertainty anymore. I wanted to call her and ask her what's up, but I have been denied access to all my electronics. I gave Mom some sob story that I needed to get an assignment from Fadia. I was like, "I'm already in a ton of trouble, do you really want me to fail English, too?" She let me use the landline. I didn't even know we had one.

Fadia answered on the first ring. "It's me, Plum," I said.

"Yeah, how are you?" Fadia asked.

"I'm okay. How are *you*?"

"Me?" Fadia sounded surprised. "I'm fine."

"Well…I wasn't sure since you didn't show up at lunch and Ollie says you've been radio silent and…"

"I've been busy," Fadia said.

"Oh, okay. So, we're cool?"

"I mean, my parents are freaked out. The rumor mill is in full effect and my Mom got the lowdown last night, so she was like, 'You don't know this troublemaker Plum Parrish, right?'"

JEN MANN

"Oh, crap. What did you say?"

"I told her she was wrong about you. I told her that her friends were wrong. I told her that there's more than one side to every story and she needs to get all sides before she passes judgment on someone she doesn't even know!"

I was shocked. Fadia talks a lot of trash behind her parents' backs and she sneaks around a lot, but she never talks to them to their faces like that. "Wow."

"You should have seen my mom. She was, like, stunned silent. My dad tried to get involved at that point and I was like, 'The two of you are on the wrong side. I was being bullied and Plum stuck up for me. No one's ever stuck up for me before.' And then I showed them the video."

I gripped the phone tighter. "What are you talking about?"

"The video I took during your smackdown."

"What?"

"I showed it to them and then I put it up on Snapchat. That was actually my dad's idea. He was like, 'Everyone should see this side of the story.' Who knew my dad could be so cool?"

"I'm so confused," I said.

"I made a video of you telling off Emberleigh. I cut it down so it's just the part where you're yelling at her and telling her to go to hell, basically. It's epic."

My stomach flip-flopped. "Oh my God, why did you do that, Fadia?"

"I don't know. It seemed like a good idea at the time. I felt like what you said spoke to me. I was, like, inspired or whatever. I put some music behind it and now you're like the fricking Mockingjay or something—I mean without the bow and arrow and the hot boyfriend, but still. I wanted it to share it with my peeps. But then…"

"What?" I asked.

"I didn't think it would happen, but it went viral."

"I'm viral?" I demanded.

"Yeah, a little bit." Fadia sounded uncomfortable. "Okay, maybe a little more than a little bit."

"How much more?"

"Umm…hang on, let me check the stats." I heard Fadia fumbling with her phone. "Two million views."

"What?!"

"But one of my sisters says those numbers are totally exaggerated and it's probably only half that, and then another sister says those numbers are super low and it's probably three times that many. Either way, at least a million people have watched it."

"Holy shit, Fadia!"

"I know, right?" Fadia giggled. "You're totally famous—Internet famous, but that's still kind of famous."

"I'm gonna puke," I said.

"Why? This is insane, but it's, like, a good insane. You're a hero, Plum."

"I don't even remember what I said to her, Fadia. It just rushed out of me. I probably didn't even make sense. Did I make sense? Did I sound stupid?"

Fadia laughed. "You didn't sound stupid."

"You're lying. I have the vocabulary of a fourth grader. It probably sucked. Plus, maybe I didn't mean some of it, y'know? I was just, like, ranting or whatever. I wasn't even trying to come up with an educated argument or whatever."

"Too late, girl, it's all you now. I set up some social media accounts, too."

"What? Why?"

"Well, because when I posted the video I didn't use your real name and people were trying to track you down and stuff, so I thought it was better to give you a pseudonym and they could follow you there. You're Queen of the Misfits on everything. You've already got a few thousand followers."

"Are you kidding me right now?" I said. "Holy shit. I need a paper bag to breathe into. What am I supposed to do now?"

"I don't know. Talk to them," Fadia said. "That's all they want. They want to be heard. To be seen. I'll send you some of the emails and you can respond if you want. Kids out there feel like they're not alone, like you spoke for them. You said what they couldn't say, either because they're afraid or they didn't know how or whatever."

"I can't even believe you did this, Fadia."

"I know. Believe me, if I knew it was going to turn into a circus, I would have totally asked you first. I had no idea it would take off like this. If you want, I can just shut it all down and you can go silent. They'll forget about you by Monday. The Internet has a short attention span."

"I don't know what to do," I said, shaking my head. "Just send the stuff over. I need to read it, and I've got to talk to my parents about it all. I'm not allowed to create new accounts on social media without their permission. I need to show them all of this."

"So don't shut it down?" Fadia asked.

"No, not until you hear from me," I said.

I spent the rest of the day reading the emails and messages.

So many of the emails were positive and encouraging:

Dear Queen,

I've never written a letter like this before to anyone, not even to T-Swift, but I had to write to you. I saw your video online and all I could think was, ME TOO! I'm picked on and harassed and teased every day and no one cares. The teachers tell me to ignore my tormentors and my parents tell me that it will be better when I'm older …

Dear QOTM,

Damn, girl, you are my IDOL! I only wish you would have punched that girl in her face. But it's good you didn't or else you'd be reading this in jail. Thank you for sticking up for the rest of us …

Dear Plum—it's Plum, right? (My neighbor's cousin's daughter goes to your school and she said your name is Plum.)

Anyway, it doesn't matter. Hi. Fellow misfit here. I've pretty much never fit in anywhere. I'm weird and I don't have a lot of social skills and I'm so quiet that I think only five people at my school know my name. Last year I found my name on a list of kids with a question mark next to it and the question: "Does she still go here?" written beside it. Sooo, what I'm trying to say is we are the same. I watched your video probably a hundred times and yelled, "Yes!" over and over again ...

Dear Queen of the Misfits,

I'm not sure what a misfit is exactly, but I'm guessing I'm one. I watched your vid and all I can say is, let's be BFFs and share clothes, OK?

A few were negative:

Dear Queen of the Misfits,

Misfit sounds about right! You are clearly a deranged human being who should be institutionalized! You attacked that poor girl for doing nothing except being better at life than you! I'm sorry that you're ugly and unpopular, but it's not her fault. Stop blaming others for your own insecurities! You're the bully!

And some were just gross:

Hey Girl,

U look yummy.

In the end, the positive outweighed the negative. I took them all to Mom and Dad.

Mom looked up from my laptop. "What have you done, Plum Parrish?" she demanded.

"Is it bad?" Dad asked, snatching the computer from her.

Mom shook her head. "It's just...wild. The Internet is a wild place, Plum. I can't believe how careless you and your friends were. You know you're not supposed to post pictures or videos of yourself on the Internet without permission."

"I know," I said. "I didn't do this. Fadia did. She recorded the whole thing and then she's the one who posted it. I didn't know she did it until just now. She had no idea it would catch on like this. I can tell her take it all down. She said the Internet has a short attention span and they'll forget about me by Monday."

Mom rubbed her eyes. "Yes, that's probably true," she agreed. "But then again, I don't know. It's not like you're doing anything wrong. What do you think, Ben?"

Dad was watching the video for the second or third time. He looked at her. "What? Oh," he hit the pause button, "I don't know either. This is a whole new territory for us."

"What is?" Pax asked, joining the conversation without being invited. He flounced on the floor and held out his hand to Dad. "What are you watching?"

Dad handed the laptop to Pax silently. We all watched Pax's face go from incredibly bored to slightly confused to downright astonished. He sat up quickly. "Plum!"

"Yes?"

"Plum, that's you! That's you telling off Emberleigh! I heard about this, but I didn't get a chance to watch yet."

"You knew about this video, Pax?" Mom asked.

Pax shrugged. "I heard some rumblings about it today, but I didn't really pay attention. I'm kind of exhausted these days from defending Plum's good name."

"You've had to defend her?" Dad asked.

"A lot," Pax said.

"I didn't know you defended me," I said. "Savannah said you hate me, too."

Pax sighed heavily. "Plum, when are you going to get it through your skull that I'm on your side? I think you bleached your brain when you wrecked your hair. I'm your brother and no one is allowed to talk smack about you when I'm around. *I* can call you a weirdo, but no one else can, y'know?"

I nodded.

He turned back to the video. "I didn't think it would be this good!"

I could feel my face turn red. "It was no big deal," I said, secretly pleased he was giving me so much praise. I didn't realize how much I'd missed my brother.

"No, no, it was a big deal. It was a *huge* deal, Plum. I don't think you understand. You told Emberleigh what everyone else has been dying to tell her since the day they met her. They've just never had the guts, but you did. You stood up for yourself and your friends, and now perfect strangers think you stood up for them, too."

"Really?" Dad said. "That's what they think?"

"I think he's right," I said. "There are a ton of emails I can show you."

"How did people get your email address?" Dad asked.

"Fadia created a new one for me: The Queen of the Misfits."

Mom winced a little. "Queen of the Misfits, huh?"

I shrugged. "I overheard you call me that once or twice and I guess it stuck."

"Plum," Mom said.

191

"It's cool," I interrupted. "I kind of like it."

"So let me get this straight," Dad said. "Fadia put up this video, millions of people watched it, she created an email address for you, and now you're getting emails from fans?"

"And some haters and a few creepers," I said.

Mom waved a hand. "Basement dwellers hacking at their keyboards with Cheetos-encrusted fingers. Ignore them!"

"So what do you want to do now, Plum?" Dad asked.

"What do you mean? I guess just let the video go and maybe answer some of the emails?"

"That's it? That's all you want to do?" Dad asked.

I was confused. "What else do you think I could do?"

"You could start making videos every week, Plum," Pax said.

"Every week? I can't go around telling off Emberleigh every week, Pax."

"No! You don't get it, do you? It's not about Emberleigh. Probably a hundred kids from SPHS watched that video. You've got millions of kids all over the country—maybe even the world—who watched that video and felt like you were telling off their *own* Emberleigh. You were being your own authentic self and they related to that. Look at these emails," he scrolled through the emails, "'We could be besties,' 'I love your approach,' 'You said what I was thinking,' 'You made me stronger.' You could talk about anything and they'd watch. Probably not all of them, but a lot of them. They just want to hear what you think, what you have to say. They're like you, Plum. They don't feel like they fit in and they feel alone. You make them feel…unalone? Is that even a word?"

"How about she makes them feel like they're not alone?" Mom said.

"Fine. You make them feel like they aren't alone," Pax said. "You understand them and they understand you."

I blinked rapidly, taking in everything Pax had just unloaded on me. I looked at my parents, who were also gaping at him. Pax doesn't normally say much beyond the occasional grunt, so we were all surprised by his brain dump.

"Pax is right," Mom said, disbelief tinged her voice. "He's absolutely right.

These kids are hurting. They're feeling like they're…"

"Weird and strange and a lot," I said.

Mom smiled. "Yes, exactly. They want to hear from you. They *need* to hear from you."

"So, we're going to let Plum make more videos?" Dad asked.

Mom looked at me. "If that's what Plum wants to do. What do you think, Plum?"

"I don't know," I whispered.

"You do you, Plum," said Dad.

I didn't say anything. I just stared at the counter on the computer screen. Every few seconds, several thousand more people watched my video. Every few seconds, several hundred more comments were left. It was daunting. It was exciting. It was terrifying. I never expected so many people to watch me or to reach out to me. To hear me. To understand me. To be moved by me. I had no idea what my next video would be about, but whatever it was, I knew it would never be as popular as that one. Without even trying I'd hit my zenith and there was really nowhere else to go but down. Was I ready for that kind of letdown right from the start? But I did like reading those emails and comments and knowing that *I* wasn't alone.

Plum's Punch List:

1. Internet creepers
2. Impostor syndrome

Thursday

September 22

I woke up to a text message from Kennedy.

Well, well, well, it took her long enough, amiright?

KENNEDY: HEY GIRL! OMG, I SAW UR VID. WTF? UR
FAMOUS AF! EVERYONE HERE IS LOSING THEIR MINDS.
NO ONE CUD BELIEVE IT WAS U, BUT I KNEW YOU HAD IT
IN U. WE SHUD MAKE A VID TOGETHER. LIKE A BFF VID.
THAT WUD B COOL, AMIRITE?

I couldn't even respond to her word salad. Kennedy's no different than Emberleigh. Actually, that's not true, Kennedy's worse. At least Emberleigh was never my friend and then dumped me when she became cooler than me and then tried to breeze back into my life again when she decided I was good enough to hang out with. Emberleigh has never tried to be my friend. She has always let me know she thought I was worthless. At least own your horrible behavior, Kennedy, y'know?

I thought about responding to Kennedy's text, but then I realized she'd given me the fodder I needed for my next video: fair-weather friends. I would reply to her, but it would be on video.

I headed downstairs, happy as a clam now that I had my next topic ready.

I was excited to tell my family and get their input when I heard Mom crying. She wasn't really loud, but I could tell it was that quiet cry she does when she was trying to keep it all bottled up so Pax and I wouldn't notice.

I heard Dad shush her. "Someone's coming," he said.

I slowed down and tried to give them some privacy, but I didn't know what to do. I needed to eat breakfast and I'd left my homework on the kitchen table. I needed to grab it before I headed to school. So, I stopped on the stairs and got busy retying my shoes and tried to give them some time to get pull themselves together.

I heard Mom blow her nose and Dad came around the corner. "Hey, Plum!" he said loudly. "How ya doing?"

I looked at him suspiciously. He hadn't been crying, but he did look guilty as hell. "Good," I said.

"Great. Your mom is…uh…"

"She's crying," I said. "I can hear her."

"Yeah," Dad said. "Yeah, she is." He looked at his feet. That's when I noticed he was wearing slippers.

Why was he wearing slippers? I wondered. I looked closer. Not only was he wearing slippers, he was wearing pajamas too. I checked my watch. It was quarter past seven. Dad always left for work at seven on the dot. "Why aren't you dressed for work?" I asked. "You sick or something?"

Pax came bounding down the stairs behind me and almost knocked me over. "Hey! Get moving, Plum," Pax said, pulling out his earbuds. "What's going on here?"

That's when Mom joined us. She was also in her slippers and pajamas (which wasn't unusual) and her face was all red and splotchy. She'd definitely been crying.

"Um, there's no easy way to say this… "Dad said.

"Oh my God! You're getting a divorce!" I cried. I flung myself at Dad. "Please don't leave us! We'll do better. I promise! I won't be so weird and Mom won't be so bossy and Pax won't be so…Pax-like!"

Dad was startled but he hugged me hard. "Plum, we're not getting divorced," he said.

"Someone's sick?" Pax asked, worry lines creased his face. "Like sick sick, not the flu or whatever?"

"Oh, jeez, Ben," Mom said. "You're scaring the crap out of them! Come sit down in the living room, you two."

Mom reached for Pax's hand and he actually took it. Dad guided me to the couch. Mom and Dad kneeled on the floor facing me and Pax.

Dad started. "So, you know how I've been working really long hours at my new job—lots of late nights and traveling a lot?"

Pax and I nodded.

"Okay, well, I was doing that because the job was really different than I expected. Right after I was hired the guy who hired me quit."

"And then this real jerk of a guy became Dad's boss," Mom said, glaring.

Dad squeezed Mom's hand. "Don't call him a jerk, Lily."

Mom snorted. "If the shoe fits."

"Loren wasn't terrific," Dad agreed.

Pax giggled. "A guy named Loren?"

I rolled my eyes. Of course Pax was losing the plot.

"Anyway," Dad continued, "Loren has been making my life pretty miserable since he took over. He's been making me work late and travel all the time. He's also been making snide remarks about how I look, what I wear, how I drive. And questioning every little thing I do. He's been…"

"Kind of bullying you?" I asked.

Dad nodded. "Well, maybe. He's so busy focusing on me and trying to catch me making a mistake that it's been stressing me out and, ironically, the stress caused me to make some mistakes."

"You dad is such a hard worker," Mom exclaimed. "He has been putting up with so much these last few weeks. You kids have no idea! This Loren is a real piece of work!"

I had been so fixated on my drama with the video and Emberleigh and now Kennedy's text message and Mom's showdown with Mrs. Davidson that I hadn't even realize how unhappy Dad was. Whether he knew it or not, he was dealing with his own bully.

"Late last night, Loren fired me," Dad said. "He finally found something

I did wrong that he could use to fire me. He called me and told me not to come in to work today."

"What?" Pax asked. "Who does that? He was just like, 'Dude, just turn off your alarm, all right? Don't even bother showing up.'"

Dad spread his hands. "Kind of? It was very abrupt. More abrupt than I expected, that's for sure. He said that cuts needed to be made and I wasn't performing the way the company expected me to and there was no sense in prolonging the inevitable and that was that. I can go in today after normal work hours and pick up my belongings."

Mom squeezed Dad's hand. "Probably because he was afraid Dad would cause a scene or something," Mom said angrily. "He would deserve it if you did! There's probably nothing there that you even want. Let them keep your plant and your daily planner!"

I know I was supposed to feel sadness, but joy spread over me. Pure unadulterated joy. Dad got fired! Now we could move back to New Jersey! Sure, I'd miss Ollie and Fadia, but we'd keep in touch and maybe I'd even stop by and see Mr. Clarence before I left. He wasn't so bad. But I was leaving! There was no way we were going to stay in Kansas now that Dad didn't have a job anymore.

"I'll start packing," I said, hopping up.

Mom shook her head and pushed me back down on the couch. "No, Plum. I know what you're thinking, but we're not moving back to New Jersey."

I was shocked. Dumbfounded. Stunned. All of it.

"We're not?" Pax asked. Even he looked a little disappointed. Who knew Perfect Pax wasn't feeling Kansas so much?

"I know it's an adjustment to be here," Dad said. "but it's really the best place for us. It's very expensive to move across the country, and we just can't afford to do it again. The job market is strong and I'll find something quickly. Until then, I get to hang out more with you two!" He did the saddest, weakest jazz hands ever.

I wasn't falling for his shenanigans. I'd heard Mom complaining to him. I knew she wanted to go back, too. "We're staying?" I asked. "Like, for real?"

Mom tried to soothe me. "Yes, Plum. It's going to be okay. You've got your friends now. And you've got your video thing to focus on. You're going to be fine here."

"We're staying?" I asked again in case I hadn't heard correctly the first time.

"Yes," Mom said. Now she was getting exasperated. "You heard us."

"Oh, come on, Mom," I said. "You can't possibly pretend like you like it here! I can see you've been crying."

"Let it go, Plum," Pax mumbled.

"No! You haven't made one friend, Mom. You want to go back, too! I know you do!" I started crying.

Mom hugged me. "I was crying because I don't like uncertainty. I like to have a plan, and right now we don't have a plan and it's freaking me out a little bit. Your dad is the stable one, Plum. His job is the one we depend upon to pay our bills with and I'm mad money. All of a sudden now, everything is on my shoulders. I'm not crying because I'm unhappy here. I'm crying because I'm worried."

I wanted to scream, "LIAR!" but I didn't. Instead I let her hug me. We rocked back and forth and cried. Pax and Dad were so uncomfortable. They just watched us and gave each other a look like, *Women! So emotional!*

I didn't even care. I let Mom hold me and I let myself cry. HARD. I knew Mom was lying, but she was doing it for me. She was doing it for Pax. And for Dad. Of course she was miserable, how could she not be? The one person she'd met in Kansas went out and found 1,000 people to sign a petition to ban her books. I ate my lunch in the bathroom a few times a month, but Mom hadn't had lunch with a friend in months. Mom didn't fit in any better than I did. In fact I would argue I was fitting in better, which was stunning. But what could she do? I could see that Dad was uneasy and I was sure she could see that, too. It was like Dad said, it was too expensive to move away, so she was going to have to work harder to support our family until he found a job. We needed to make the best of it, and she was determined to lead the way. So she was doing what she does best. She was putting on a good front for all of us. She was being strong for everyone (even if she didn't feel very strong inside) and I needed to let her do it.

I sighed heavily and wiped my snotty nose on my sleeve. "Okay," I said. "If you're not unhappy, then neither am I."

"It's going to be fine," Mom promised.

"Totally," I said.

If she can tell white lies, so can I.

Or could I? I'd been telling so many white lies over the last few weeks to spare everyone's feelings, but especially Mom's. What about my feelings? What about how I was feeling? I'd finally started speaking up for myself, defending myself, owning my behavior, and now I was going to tamp that down with a lie? I was going to push those feelings into my gut and never speak of them again so just Mom would feel a tiny bit better? Was that right? Was that what I should do? I was so confused. Mom says, "You do you," but does she really mean that?

I cleared my throat. "Actually," I said. "I'm not *not* unhappy."

"What?" Mom asked.

"That didn't come out right," I said. "I said I wasn't unhappy, but that's not true. I *am* unhappy. I'm really pissed off that we have to stay here. I'm furious that Dad got fired and that you feel pressure to bring home the money now. I am livid with Pax and his ability to fit in with any group of kids at school. And I am so irritated with myself because I'm a phony!"

"How are you a phony?" Dad asked.

"I'm a phony because all of these people watched a perfectly edited thirty-second video of me and now they think I'm some girl who has her shit together when I really don't. Everyone's going to figure out that I'm an impostor. That I'm a girl who eats her lunch in the bathroom and couldn't convince 250 people to sign a stupid petition. I'm a girl who is called names and pushed around. And I've been fooling myself, because I blamed it all on Kansas. I kept telling myself that if we went back to Jersey, everything would be better there, but I'm not sure that's true. I was an outcast in Jersey, too. Kennedy would have dumped me by now, and even Madame O'Malley might have suggested I find someone else to hang out with on Friday nights. I've always been a loser, and I've lied to myself about it. I've lied about everything.

I lied to you guys and to Mr. Clarence. I can't keep lying. Not even white lies."

"No one wants you to lie," Mom said, reaching for my hand.

I shook her off. "You're right. I'm done lying. It's time to own who I am. I'm an angry, sarcastic, annoying girl who is a lot to handle. But I'm going to figure out how to like that girl even if no one else does."

"I like you," Pax said softly. "I should have introduced you to kids at school. I knew you weren't adjusting, but to be honest, I wasn't doing so hot myself. It's been hard breaking in with these kids. And I'm sad, too. I'm sad we're not going back to New Jersey."

"Really?" Dad asked.

Pax nodded. "Yeah, really. I realize that I'm not as emotional as Plum, but you have no idea how tough it is around here. The kids at school are so cliquey, and it's hard enough to make them think I'm worth hanging out with. It was hard to bring you in, too, Plum. But I should have tried."

"Oh," I said.

"And if we're being honest, which it sounds like we're doing, then I'll say that I'm jealous of your friendship with Ollie and Fadia."

"What?"

"Yeah. The three of you are super close. Those two are really good friends to you, Plum. You can actually talk to them and they hear you and they listen to you. My friends aren't friends. They're just dudes that I talk about sports with. I don't have any good friends here. I have a lot of acquaintances."

Pax's confession was such a shock to hear. I just assumed he fit in seamlessly and never even stressed a bit. I mean, it sucked to know he wasn't making friends, but I also felt a small tinge of happiness. For once I did something better than Pax. Yes!!!

"You can sit with us if you want to," I said. "At lunch and stuff."

"Thanks," Pax mumbled.

"Look," Mom said, "I know it's not ideal for any of us, but we're going to have to make it work. Going forward the four of us are a team, okay? We all look out for one another and we stick together, because we're all each other has. We're going to be just fine!"

"Yes, we are," Dad said, pulling us all into a group hug.

"Sure," said Pax.

"Of course," I said, crossing my fingers behind my back.

Yeah, I know, I know. I had literally just promised to stop lying, but let me tell you, it's hard to stop once you start. Plus, I didn't want to spoil the mood. Everyone was all, "Rah, rah, rah! We're a family who tells the truth and owns our feelings and sticks together!" And I was all, "How soon can we stop with the group hug?"

I have a lot to work on and I *will* do it, but it's going to take some baby steps before I'm ready to sing "Kumbaya" with the whole fam damily, y'know?

In the meantime, if you'll excuse me, I have a video to make.

Plum's Punch List:

1. Loren
2. Staying in Kansas
3. White lies
4. Group hugs

Acknowledgments

Thank you to my kids, Gomer and Adolpha, for demanding I write a book you're allowed to read. This was a lot of fun and I enjoyed having your input and getting to share this experience with you. I love you! (I know, eww, so embarrassing, Mom.)

Thank you to my editor, Hollie, who was the first person to let me know that she laughed at this book. It is always a fear of mine, that I'm the only person who finds me funny. So, thank you for that.

Thank you to my beta readers, Jessica, Leila, and Kim. You ladies made me realize that I'm a craptastic beta reader. The notes you gave were amazing and I appreciate that you took time out to help me.

Thank you to the Hubs for always believing in me and pushing me try new things. I love you! (I know, eww, so embarrassing, Jen. Get a room.)

Thank you to my Throat Punch readers. You made my dreams come true and now maybe you can share this book with your kids??

About the Author

JEN MANN is best known for her wildly popular and hysterical blog People I Want to Punch in the Throat. She has been described by many as Erma Bombeck—with f-bombs. Jen is known for her hilarious rants and funny observations on everything from parenting to gift giving to celebrity behavior to politics to Elves on Shelves. She does not suffer fools lightly. Jen is the author of the *New York Times* bestseller *People I Want to Punch in the Throat: Competitive Crafters, Drop-Off Despots, and Other Suburban Scourges* which was a Finalist for a Goodreads Reader's Choice Award. She is also the mastermind behind the New York Times bestselling *I Just Want to Pee Alone* anthology series.

This is her first book for young adults.

Jen is a married mother of two children whom she calls Gomer and Adolpha in her writings—she swears their real names are actually worse.

Find her on Facebook, Twitter, and Instagram. She doesn't do Snapchat because she's too old for that nonsense.

Notes from the Author

Thank you for reading this book. I appreciate your support and I hope you enjoyed it. I hope you will tell a friend—or 30 about this book. Please do me a huge favor and leave me a review on Amazon and Goodreads. Of course I prefer 5-star, but I'll take what I can get. If you hated this book, you can skip the review, it's cool.

Made in the USA
Lexington, KY
20 April 2017